TERMINAL

SARAH STONE BOOK 4

IAIN ROB WRIGHT

*To Sarah's patient fans –
Thanks for waiting.*

"Should we fear hackers? Intention is at the heart of this discussion."
   – Kevin Mitnick

"What atonement is there for blood spilt upon the earth?"
   – Aeschylus

"Looks like I picked the wrong week to stop sniffing glue."
   – **Steve, Airplane! (1980, Paramount Pictures)**

CHAPTER ONE

The drizzly day reminded Maxim of the tiny hamlet of Serov where he had grown up. Next to the Kakva river, it had often been raining there, but it was something he had enjoyed as an impoverished child. The rain sent people running from the streets, but not him. He would take strolls during the bad weather, convincing himself that the entire empty world belonged to him. He did not run from the rain like everybody else. God himself would not make him.

Man who walks in rain travels further than one who takes shelter.

Maxim often missed his homeland of Russia, the wide-open spaces and implacable spirit of its people, but he did not miss Putin or his cronies, who had made home such a dangerous place for men like Maxim – ambitious men unwilling to have their destinies dictated to them. The United Kingdom was now his homeland, a country ruled by a weak administration and pitiful laws. Here, a man could get away with murder if he knew the right people to threaten or bribe. This was an island of cowards with big mouths and weaklings with high chins, both crumbling at the sight of a clenched fist.

Or the barrel of a well-oiled Makarov.

With a grim, tight-lipped smile, Maxim stepped out of the drizzle and into the stale-smelling waiting room of the garage he owned – one of several in London and the South East. If anybody stuck their nose in, they would find a perfectly legitimate business. Only the most bothersome would discover the delightful sins buried within.

Today, the garage was acting as a meeting place and a refuge from the wintery drizzle.

Maxim wiped the rain from his shoulders and removed his grey woollen overcoat. He draped it across the back of a worn leather sofa that stood beneath the garage's single lead-lined front window. Opposite the large leather sofa was a smaller two-seater, and it was here that a middle-aged man sat cross-legged, impatiently waiting for Maxim's arrival.

"Councillor Hutchinson. It is good to see you."

The man stood to greet Maxim, peering at him from behind a pair of Versace spectacles. Counterfeit eyewear was one of Maxim's many income streams, so he knew most brands at a glance.

Councillor Hutchinson offered a limp handshake that Maxim ignored. "My good friend, Maxim. You're a little late, and I'm very busy, so can we move this right along to why you asked to meet with me... here." He looked around, gaze settling on a dog-eared poster of a topless tennis player. He couldn't keep himself from sniffing disdainfully.

Maxim moved over to the coffee machine at the room's edge. Picking up a chipped mug from the table, he poured himself a dose of heady Colombian blend that he had sourced for himself specially. Coffee was his one vice. Vodka, the nectar of his people, he could take or leave. Drugs and tobacco left him feeling polluted. Oh, but piping hot coffee put fire in his veins and a spring in his step.

He kept his back turned to the other man as he sipped the scalding brew, and when he eventually deigned to speak, he did so indifferently, and with a purposefully thickened accent. "I believe you know why you are here, Councillor. You are yet to accept bid for town maintenance contract."

Councillor Hutchinson chuckled, but Maxim sensed the man's nervousness, the anxious flicker behind his expensive spectacles.

"Maxim – my friend – you don't have the means to fulfil such a contract. The town's maintenance requirements are vast. The contract requires a long-established company with experience of meeting such obligations. My constituents are expecting me to—"

Maxim spun around and thrust out an arm. He seized the councillor by the throat and caused the man to yelp. Iron bars inside of Maxim twisted, and a violent beast dwelling in the pit of his stomach – the furious *chort* bred through a lifetime of adversity – broke free. "It is *you* who does not understand, Councillor. You give contract to me or your blood oils engines in my garage. Do you forget how many of your dirty little secrets I keep? The women? The drugs? And what else? It is time for you to repay my loyalty, *my friend*."

The councillor's face reddened. Maxim continued squeezing his larynx until his eyes bulged like little frogs baking in the sun. "It... It's not possible. The contract is too b-big. It would... expose us both. You... You can't—"

Maxim squeezed harder and cut off the councillor's words. "You leave everything to me. I will fulfil contract – you have my word – so do not let it be concern, okay? Sign off on bid. I will not ask again." He loosened his grip and offered a handshake. "Let us be partners."

"I... I can't. It would need approval. More than just mine."

While Maxim had been squeezing the councillor's windpipe with one hand, he had continued clutching his piping hot coffee in the other. Now he brought the chipped mug up and tossed the contents in the councillor's face, causing him to scream like a little girl. He grabbed at his face and staggered around the room.

He is lucky I do not peel his face off with wood plane as I did Vassili Bokov back in Orsk. Now that was a good time.

After a few moments, Maxim grabbed the councillor again. This time, he hurled the man down on the old leather sofa beneath the window and punched him in the stomach, turning his girlish screams into a low, guttural moan. Then he grabbed the councillor by the back of the head and brought their faces close together. "You have three days, Councillor. Three days, before wife find out man she marry. Three days, before voters learn truth about weasel they put in power. Three days, before two large men visit your daughter in night and make a woman. You think you are powerful man? You are damselfly buried in shit on boot heel."

The terrified councillor struggled to catch his breath. He was crying like a child and trembling. His maroon cheeks were blistering. At some point, his Versace glasses had fallen from his face. "I-I-I understand. Y-You'll have the contract, I promise. I promise. Just don't involve my family."

Maxim grabbed the councillor by the hand and pulled him to his feet, initiating a handshake that finally made contact. The dance was over. "Then we are partners, yes? We should celebrate. You want coffee?"

The councillor attempted to straighten himself up, but it was little more than a pathetic charade with his bright red, scalded face and dismayed expression. "Um, no, thank you. I think I've had enough."

Maxim smiled amiably and patted the councillor hard on the back. "You be good to Maxim, and Maxim be good to you. Always shall it be. Now go, my friend. Fly out of here like shit-covered damselfly."

The councillor fled into the drizzling rain. Maxim chuckled at the sight of a grown man running in terror. It was something he himself would never do.

Better to face wolf than run like rabbit.

Maxim knelt to grab something that glinted beneath the sofa

– the councillor's Versace spectacles. Maxim tried them on, but sneered when he found a prescription strong enough to allow a naked mole rat to see. He tossed the spectacles back onto the floor and trod on them, enjoying the minor act of destruction and the symbolic gesture of crushing another human being's ego and self-worth.

The councillor had, of course, been correct in his concerns. There was no way Maxim's current businesses could handle the town's vast maintenance needs, but that was beside the point. He would hire the cheapest firm capable of meeting the contract and pocket the difference for himself. It was another guaranteed income stream – and another hook Maxim had planted in local government. Once again, his influence grew.

This game is too easy.

From filthy gutters to a throne of my own making, that is my destiny.

One day, even Putin will fear me.

Maxim poured himself another coffee, this time with milk.

CHAPTER TWO

"Okay, I'm getting a little nauseated staring at your faces for so long, so I'll wrap this up." Sarah allowed a smirk to bother the edges of her mouth, but she kept her expression stern. The seven men and women standing shoulder to shoulder in front of her were fine agents, but they were also her underlings, which meant she had the right to abuse them a little bit. "To summarise" – she whacked her pointer against the ninety-inch projection screen on the wall behind her, displaying a blown-up image of the United Kingdom's South East – "this Russian Mafia offshoot goes by the name *Novaya Sila* – new power – and we should focus our efforts on its leader, Maxim Ivanov. He's been in the country for two years, and in that time, he has set up or purchased approximately thirty-five businesses. He owns garages, shops, taxi firms, and more. All fronts for what he's really into, of course, which is everything. Illegal imports, firearms, drugs, extortion, blackmail, murder for hire, and probably failing to wipe his hands after taking a shit. He is bad news, which is why we want him locked up or sent somewhere else." She glanced at her scuffed Sekonda and folded away her pointer. "Okay, it's afternoon, so to summarise further: Russian crime syndicate bad. Let's not allow it to get any worse. All right, children, get back to work."

The agents broke away, shuffling out of the briefing room and heading for their workspaces. The briefing room was one of four inside the earthworm's middle section, each filled with rows of chairs and a large projector screen. The MCU was high tech, but sometimes all you needed was PowerPoint and a tappy stick.

Thomas and Jessica leant against the wall at the back of the room, arms folded. The director and deputy director of the MCU regularly sat in on Sarah's briefings, and she hated it. She loathed being questioned or appraised in any way. It was something she had been working on for several years now, but bad habits were hard to break.

I'll always be a work in progress.

Or a finished Picasso. I have the face for it.

Thomas attempted to speak, but Sarah cut him off. "I can already see you have a problem, so what is it?"

With a smirk on his clean-shaven face, showing he was combative but not angry, Thomas said, "You already know how I view this operation. Let the uniforms deal with petty crime. We need to keep our eye on the bigger picture. This is a waste of resources."

Sarah pouted and stamped her feet. "Aw, shucks, but I'm so bored with terrorism, Pa. Once you seen one idiot with a bomb, you seen 'em all."

"You know I'm from Florida, right?"

She stopped play-acting. "This isn't just petty crime we're talking about, Thomas. Maxim Ivanov is a player, and if we don't deal with him now, he'll be a thorn in our sides later. He's got his grubby fingers in way too many pies, and I'm taking it personally."

Jessica chuckled. She was wearing her lab coat as usual but had her silky brown hair down for a change. "You take *everything* personally, sweetheart, but I happen to agree with you. Terrorism will always be our chief priority, and we have two-thirds of the MCU dedicated to stopping it, so let's branch out a little. Evil is evil, after all. And like my sweet Aunt May used to say, 'better to pull the root than the weed.' Let's stop Ivan Maximov before he has a chance to cause us bigger problems later."

Sarah cleared her throat. "Maxim Ivanov."

"That's what I said, sweetheart."

Sarah gave Jessica an appreciative nod. While they didn't always see eye to eye, the good doctor was a close friend of hers and someone she trusted. Her relationship with Thomas, however, was far more complex. Working alongside her ex-husband, once presumed dead, was more stressful than any terrorist plot could be.

Thomas put his hands up to placate Sarah. "You know I would never tell you what to do – I wouldn't dare – so I'll just warn you to be mindful of using up too many resources on this, okay? The Russian Mafia is someone else's fish to catch." Sarah went to argue, and possibly insult Thomas for good measure, but he didn't allow her to speak. "Let me be your boss for one minute, okay? Nod and show me you at least heard what I said."

Sarah nodded.

Thomas clapped his hands together. "Fantastic! Now, do you fancy getting some lunch? I've been on duty for sixteen hours. I'm gonna grab some lunch and hit the hay. Company would be nice though."

"Thought you wanted to be my boss. Now you're asking me on a date?"

"Okay, fine. We can invite Jessica, too, if it makes my presence more palatable."

Jessica waved a hand. "Not for me, thanks. I had a mighty breakfast. Y'all go grab something together. I'll hold the fort."

Sarah allowed her shoulders to sag. Like Thomas, she'd been on duty for way too many hours, and her body was pleading with her to collapse inside one of the earthworm's many dorm rooms.

She wanted to sleep the day away, but it might be a good idea to eat something first. "All right, but I'm choosing where we eat."

Thomas smiled as if he had just won a great battle, but the reality was far from it. Sarah might be willing to talk to him these days, but the past was still a jagged fingernail stuck between her teeth. Try as she might, she couldn't dislodge it.

My anger is fading, though.

When did I stop hating him?

"I'll meet you up top in ten minutes," he said. Then he and Jessica left the briefing room. Sarah waited a moment before exiting herself, wanting to be alone with her thoughts for a moment. There was a lot going on right now, and all of it was complicated. Last year had seen her fortieth birthday and she suddenly felt old. While her body had once been a tool at her complete command, it now refused to do everything it was told. Everything she did was a few microseconds slower, just a little bit stiffer.

How much longer can I keep this up?

There was nothing urgent to take care of, so Sarah grabbed her grey denim jacket and pulled it on over her white button-down shirt. She exited her office and headed for the lifts. Usually she took the stairs – the healthier option – but she was too weary right now. The doors opened directly onto the tarmac, where a small landing strip housed a pair of Cessna 210s and the old Griffin helicopter that had first brought Sarah to the MCU a lifetime ago. A covered carpool contained more than seventy-five vehicles. The earthworm's facilities had expanded greatly over the last decade, at the cost of half a billion pounds.

We started at the bottom, now we are here.

As usual, the MCU's senior driver, Mandy, was pottering around inside the carpool, running a chamois leather over the bonnet of a creamy white, newly registered Alfa Romeo Giulia. While Jaguars and Range Rovers made up a majority of the fleet – symbols of British prowess – various other models had been added in recent years.

"Hey, Mandy," she said, waving a hand. "How's it going?"

Mandy looked at Sarah glumly and failed to smile. "Do we have a mission?"

She perched on the sleek bonnet of a nearby Jaguar XJ saloon. "Nope. Just gunna grab some lunch. You want me to bring you back anything?"

He went back to his polishing. "Not much of an appetite lately."

"I understand."

The tragedy had occurred nearly two months ago now, but Mandy was taking it hard. He'd stopped coming down into the earthworm and spent most of his time alone in the carpool. The expensive vehicles were apparently better company than people. "We all miss Howard," she said. "It sucks that he's gone."

Mandy kept his back turned, buffing the Giulia's bonnet. "I can't accept it. I keep trying to make peace with it, to let it bed in, but it doesn't feel real. How haven't we caught the person who did it? All the resources at our disposal, Sarah, and we can't even—"

"You'll get your answers, Mandy, I promise. Just be patient." She hated having to placate him with empty assurances, but she didn't know what else to say. Law enforcement was seeking the driver of an old SUV, possibly a Mitsubishi, but had so far come up empty-handed. The vehicle had reportedly mowed down senior MCU agent Howard Hopkins as he crossed a road in Camden. He hadn't even been on duty. He'd been Christmas shopping.

"We need to work harder," said Mandy. "I won't rest while his murderer walks around free. He deserves better."

"I miss him too, Mandy. Howard's the whole reason I'm even here. He gave my life meaning when I thought it was over."

"Then you shouldn't be okay."

"I'm not okay. Believe me."

Mandy didn't look at her, but he nodded silently.

"I'm here if you need to talk, okay?"

Mandy sighed and finally turned back to face her. He looked ready to shed a tear, which would be obscene on a face as large as his. The giant of a man had a soft heart but behaved as though he considered it a weakness. "Sure, I'll be driving you somewhere soon," he said. "Maybe we'll talk then."

"Sure thing, Mandy. I'll always need you behind the wheel. Hey..." She chuckled. "Remember when Howard got taken hostage by Dr Cartwright? I thought he was going to piss his pants."

"We really dropped the ball that day, didn't we? It was your first mission."

Sarah remembered it well, the surreal nightmare that had changed her life. "We got the bad guys in the end, though, didn't we? We always do."

"But sometimes they get *us*. Bradley, Palu, and now Howard. I'm tired of losing people, Sarah." He straightened up and peered down at her. "You keep yourself safe, do you hear me?"

Faced with his unrelenting stare, Sarah blushed. "Yeah, I hear you. Look, um, I want to tell you something, okay? Just promise me that you'll—"

"Thought I'd find you here," said Thomas, weaving between the cars towards them. "You picked out a ride yet?"

Sarah shook her head. "No."

Mandy tapped the Alfa Romeo's roof. "Take the Giulia. Just gave her a clean." He tossed the key fob into the air and Thomas caught it.

"Italian beauty," he said with a grin. "Can't beat it." He strolled over to the car and the door locks disengaged automatically. Opening the front passenger door, he motioned for Sarah to get in. "Although there's plenty to be said for a fine English rose."

Sarah rolled her eyes. "There's nothing fine about me, unless you like disfigured, bad-tempered old women." She dumped herself into the passenger seat and pulled up her legs. Her feet throbbed inside her scruffy black combat boots.

"Just so happens that's exactly what I'm into." Thomas shut her door and trotted around to the driver's side, sliding behind the wheel and switching on the engine. The V6's demonic roar aroused Sarah in ways no man ever had, and she closed her eyes to enjoy it. Life as a senior agent in the MCU certainly had its perks.

Thomas turned to Sarah and allowed his stare to linger a second longer than was comfortable. "So, where to? You said you wanted to choose the place we ate."

She shrugged. "Burger King?"

Thomas rolled his eyes and gripped the undersized steering wheel. "You're all class, lady. How 'bout we go grab a pizza at Vee's?"

Sarah slumped back into the seat's red-stitched nappa leather. "Whatever. Let's just eat fast so we can get to bed."

Thomas winked at her. "Now you're talking my language. Your place or mine?"

"Don't push your luck. You're lucky I'm even willing to eat with you."

Thomas thickened his accent to stereotypical levels and said, "Bussin food and a fine gal for conversation. I'm gone take that to the bank."

"Like I was saying, don't push your luck, pardner."

"Again, you know I'm from Florida, right?"

"I surely do."

Thomas shook his head and tittered, then put the Giulia in gear. He crept the saloon's sleek bonnet forwards, navigating between the row upon row of other vehicles. "Hey," he said, "I'm glad we can finally be friends."

"Me too, because I have more than enough enemies." She looked out of the window at the grey February sky.

Enough to keep me awake at night.

. . .

Oliver Simpson stumbled out of his bedroom, unable to decide whether to go downstairs or into the bathroom to vomit. His stomach was a clenched fist. The glands in his throat bulged like a pufferfish. It was a battle just to stay standing. In the bedroom behind him, his computer chirped as it completed its shutdown routine. He wondered if he would ever dare switch it on again.

What have I done?

Calm down. Everything is going to be okay.

Oliver braved the stairs and tried to behave normally. Already dressed for work, he went into the kitchen and readied himself to go catch the bus, pouring himself a glass of water and leaning over the counter with it. He took small sips until he felt less nauseated.

"Are you okay, honey?" His mum entered the kitchen behind him, obviously recognising he was unwell. He could never hide even the smallest of sniffles from her. She put her hand on his back and rubbed. "What's the matter, buttercup?"

He turned to face her, forcing himself to smile. The last thing he wanted was to tell her what had just happened, so he didn't. How could he even explain it? She wouldn't understand, even if he tried to make her. "I-I'm fine. Just feeling a bit sick, that's all."

It was 11 a.m., but his mum was in her old pink dressing gown and silk pyjamas. Some days, she didn't bother getting dressed at all. She placed the back of her hand against his forehead and tutted. "You're as pale as a ghost. Have you been spending too much time on that computer? You need to stop and get some fresh air every couple of hours, honey. I read that the other day in the—" She stopped and eyed him suspiciously. "You haven't been watching something you shouldn't have, have you?" She was referring to the time Oliver had downloaded a beheading video. It had affected him badly for over a week. Sometimes he still thought about it.

He swatted her hand away from his forehead. "I was just playing a game."

"Flying your planes?"

He shook his head. "No. Something else."

To make matters worse, his dad walked into the kitchen and joined them. He was bleary-eyed and yawning, wearing mismatched socks and Homer Simpson boxer shorts. The thick black hair on his belly tumbled over the fraying waistband. "You want to get out and play some footie, son. I went semi-professional at your age. Messing around on flight simulators and watching porn all day isn't healthy. You turn eighteen in a month; time to get out and enjoy the world, because life's too short."

Oliver rolled his eyes. He didn't see how playing football would improve his life. The entire world ran on computers, so spending time on a keyboard seemed a better use of time than kicking a bag of wind. Although, right now, he never wanted to look at a computer again. "I'm fine, okay? I feel sick, but it's easing off."

His mum shook her head. "I'll call the doctor. Better to be sure."

"I'm fine."

"You never know. What if you have—"

"No, Mum. Don't get carried away. I'm not... I'm just..." He let out a breath, trying to ease the pounding in his chest. "I'm okay. All right?"

She looked away. "Fine. I just worry."

"I know you do, but don't." He sighed, then gulped the last of his water before placing the glass upside down in the sink. Wiping his mouth with the back of his hand, he tried to resist the urge to retch. "I need to go to work now. I'll see you when I get back."

His dad shook his head. "You won't. I'm working the late shift tonight. Matthew called in sick again. Probably won't be back until the early hours. That place will be the death of me."

Oliver didn't disagree. His dad seemed to spend every waking hour at the chippie lately, and most people didn't even want fish and chips any more. People at school were always winding Oliver up about his dad's business. They said he stank of pickled eggs. "I'll catch you in the morning then."

"Maybe we can go out for breakfast? How's a full English at Trotter's sound?"

Oliver's mum smacked her lips. "Sounds good to me."

Eating was the last thing on Oliver's mind, but he forced himself to smile – like his parents constantly did to him. "Yeah, okay, breakfast."

"Great." His dad patted him on the shoulder and cupped the back of his neck. "Have a good day at work, son. I can't believe how grown-up you are. It seems like only yesterday that... Well, you know."

Oliver nodded. "I have to go."

"Come home if you don't feel better," his mum added.

"I will. See you both later."

His mum reached in for a hug, and for once he allowed it. In fact, a cuddle from her was something he wanted very much.

Maybe I should tell her. Tell her what I did.

I was only messing around. I didn't mean it.

She would never understand. Dad will kill me.

"I, um, love you both."

That was an odd thing for him to say, and it clearly startled his parents.

"We love you too, buttercup."

"And we always will." His dad shifted awkwardly as he said it. "You best get going. Don't want to be late."

"Yeah, okay. Bye." Oliver turned to exit the kitchen, but his mum suddenly grabbed him by the shoulders. "Honey, you're trembling. Are you sure you're okay?"

He pulled away and turned towards the kitchen door. "I already told you, I'm fine. Get off my back about it, okay?"

"All right, no need to get stroppy. See you for a late dinner?"

"I'll be back around six." In the hallway he grabbed his house keys from the dish on top of the radiator cover and headed for the front door. For a moment, he envisioned flashing lights at the end of the driveway, but he forced himself to push the fear aside.

He turned and glanced into the mirror set above the radiator. His flesh was pale, eyes red.

I'm so fucked.

He headed to work, wondering how long he had before they came for him.

Maxim pulled his Maserati to a skidding halt at the side of the highway and stepped out onto the verge. It was a dangerous place to park, but he needed to deal with this situation at once. He pulled out the mobile phone he was using that day and dialled the number of his contact, a man who owed his life to Maxim.

"Thomas? I demand answers. One of my shipments has been seized at Dover, and I understand the MCU is responsible. Do you have no control over your people?" He squeezed the phone so hard that the plastic creaked in his ear. "This investigation into my business needs to stop immediately, do you hear me? I will tolerate no more interference." He listened as Thomas gave excuses and explanations, but after ten seconds Maxim could take no more. He bellowed into the mouthpiece. "Quiet! I did not pull you out of desert and give you back life just to have you abandon your obligations to me. We have deal. A lot of my money is in your pockets, so do what I pay you for, or I will bury you so deep in ground that no one will ever find you."

Maxim wasn't interested in hearing a response, so he ended the call and put the phone back in his pocket.

He had been en route to Dover to pay off various officials and check on his latest shipment of imported superbikes when he had received a warning from one of his people. MCU agents and port security had seized the shipment and arrested the couriers. None of the thirty expensive motorcycles had come into the country legally – import duties were unpaid – and now that they had been seized, it was only a matter of time before law enforcement found the bags of heroin stuffed inside the mufflers. Maxim had lost half a million pounds in high-spec Japanese motorcycles and three times as much in drugs. A bad day.

But such is the cost of doing business.

A spider that loses leg still hunts fly.

As expensive a setback as it might have been, today's bust also presented an opportunity. It was a chance to discover who in his organisation was unreliable or incompetent. The American, Thomas Gellar, had so far been a useful asset, concealing Maxim's association with the deceased terrorist Al Al-Sharir and erasing evidence of several misdeeds that might otherwise have come back to haunt him, but today's failure was unacceptable. That the MCU was executing a campaign targeted directly at Maxim was crime enough, but the MCU's director being in his back pocket made it even less forgivable.

Thomas needs to get a handle on this at once.

Perhaps I should take care of problem myself. All I need is name of whoever is pushing so hard to investigate me. A simple bullet to back of the brain solves many problems.

Maxim slid his mobile phone back out of his pocket and made another call. This time he called his people in Calais, ordering them to hold tight on any further shipments. Things needed to pause while Thomas Gellar did his job.

Or until I take care of him.

And whoever else stands in my way.

A minivan rolled to a stop behind Maxim's Maserati. A man in a turban popped his head out of the window and smiled. "Need some help, chief? I'm a mechanic."

Maxim pulled out his walnut-gripped Colt Python, taken ten years ago from a dead soldier in Chechnya, and pointed it at the Good Samaritan. "I do not need mechanic, or a Sikh. So fuck off or die."

The minivan sped back onto the highway, tyres screeching.

Maxim put his weapon away and swore in Russian. "Stupid

Maxim. Let your enemies lose their heads, but you must keep yours."

The Sikh would call the police, so it was time to go. No sense in making a bad day worse. Better to concentrate on punishing those responsible.

Maxim climbed back behind the wheel of his Maserati and thought about who to kill.

CHAPTER THREE

Before they had even ordered drinks, Thomas slipped away to take a phone call. He came back a few minutes later, looking distracted and worried. He placed his phone on the table and nudged it away, as if it smelled bad.

"Everything okay?" Sarah asked him. She was holding a menu but hadn't looked at it yet. Her stomach rumbled at the thought of eating.

He picked up the other menu with his hands trembling. "I'm starving. What are you having?"

"Not sure yet. I don't want a full stomach before I sleep." She studied the menu and found the sandwich list. "Think I'll just go for the three-cheese pitta. Maybe get some fries to share?"

Thomas still appeared distracted. He glanced at the menu but didn't seem to take it in. Eventually, he placed it flat on the table. "I'll have the same as you. I'll flag a waiter." He turned around. Sarah reached forward and grabbed his phone. Three seconds later, he turned back and caught her with it. "What are you doing?"

Sarah fiddled with the phone and then placed it back down on the table. "Being nosey. Who were you on the phone to? Why are you so distracted?"

He grabbed his phone and put it in his pocket. Rather than annoyed, he seemed worried by her impropriety. "It was just the Pentagon wanting to know how we're spending their money. Shall I order or not?"

"Sure." Sarah leant back in her chair while Thomas clicked his fingers to get the attention of a nearby waitress. It was a rude gesture, and Sarah saw the disdain flash across the young girl's face. Hopefully, she would only spit in Thomas's pitta.

"Are you ready to order, sir?"

Thomas gave the waitress their order and she went away to fetch them drinks. Thomas turned back to Sarah, slightly more at ease. Perhaps he was just tired. She felt pretty jittery herself.

"Just like old times, huh?" he said. "Having dinner together."

"It's lunch, but I suppose it *is* like old times – except we're not in the desert and nobody's shooting at us. Also, this place is cleaner than Camp Bastion's NAAFI, and while I haven't checked the toilets, I assume there's less piss on the floor."

Thomas chuckled. He picked up his knife and fork and started tapping them gently against the table. He'd always been a fidgeter, and Sarah remembered how it used to annoy her back when they'd shared a bed. "You seem anxious, Tom. Is everything all right?"

He exhaled until his lungs were empty then refilled them. "I could use a break, to be honest. It's been a few years since I've been home. I've been avoiding it."

Sarah frowned. Florida wasn't a place to avoid, in her mind. In fact, it was a sun-drenched paradise – a paradise she'd once nearly made her home. "What do you mean?"

Thomas shrugged. "Whenever I go home, it reminds me of all the hopes and dreams I used to have but never made true. It's home, but at the same time it's not. Life doesn't end up the way you plan it, does it?"

"Seven years ago, I imagined I'd end my life on the living room floor surrounded by pills and vodka. Never dreamt I'd end up here. The MCU has changed me in ways I can't undo. The past is like something I dreamed. If you're struggling with the decisions you've made, just remind yourself that you made them for what you thought were the right reasons."

He smiled but couldn't look her in the eye. "I thought you hated me for the decisions I've made."

"Maybe we're both different people than we used to be."

"Does that mean we can start again? Put the past behind us?"

Sarah swallowed. Thomas made no secret of his desire of restarting a relationship with her, but it didn't change how much he had hurt her. The concept of forgiving him had never crossed her mind. He was guilty of too much. "Thomas, I..."

The waitress placed their drinks down on the table with a fake smile. "Your sandwiches will be right with you," she said.

Thomas nodded and waved her away. Another rude gesture that would surely cement the young girl's intention of spitting in his pitta. Once again, Sarah hoped she wasn't found guilty by association. She took a sip from her orange juice tentatively.

Thomas leant forward, eyes wide and focused only on her. "What were you about to say?"

"I'm too tired to have a complicated conversation right now. Can we just talk about something else?"

He slumped back in his chair. "Okay, fine. Any leads on the hit-and-run driver? I have Howard's mother on the line every day asking for updates. She's going to make me insane."

"Jesus, Thomas, I said I didn't want a complicated conversation. You reckon, maybe, that Howard's death might be a little too heavy for a light lunch?"

"Sorry, you're right. Hard to talk about anything other than work though. You think we should get lives beyond the MCU?"

"Now there's a thought. I could finally take up ballet and make my father happy. God rest his rotten soul."

"Such a shame I never got to meet the esteemed Major Stone. He raised a pretty exceptional daughter."

"Flattery will get you everywhere."

"You're beautiful."

She flinched. "I'm disfigured."

Thomas shook his head and stared into her eyes. "Not to me. Never to me."

"Tom, just stop it, okay? I can't do this right—"

He reached across the table for her hand. She couldn't decide, in the moment, whether to pull away or not.

Their phones both rang at the same time.

Sarah sat up straight and pulled the Samsung from her inside pocket. She had a special ringtone for Jessica, so she knew it was her before she answered. "Jess? What's up? Whoa, whoa, whoa, calm down. Jesus, are you kidding me?"

Sarah listened as her colleague rambled down the phone. Thomas's expression grew ugly at the same time as hers. He was taking a similar call. Sarah could barely believe what she was hearing.

Five hundred dead. Final tally unknown.

A fresh disaster had befallen the United Kingdom.

Sleep would have to wait.

The waitress brought over their pittas, but by then Sarah and Thomas were already rushing out of the restaurant.

The drive to Watford took less than an hour, mainly thanks to Thomas pushing the Alfa's speedometer past ninety for most of the journey. When they reached the town, they manoeuvred through a police cordon and headed towards flashing lights. A billowing black smoke cloud cut through the bleak afternoon sky, and they saw it long before they reached their eventual destination.

Thomas parked in a side street outside a bakery. The shop's large front window had shattered, and the scent of freshly baked bread wafted out and mixed with the odour of burning metal. A sour taste filled Sarah's mouth. This was going to be a bad one.

I can feel the death.

Am I developing a sixth sense for misery?

She and Thomas exchanged glances as they got out of the car. They walked in silence towards the area of town where Mattock and his team would be waiting for them. The disaster had struck a supermarket off the A411. It was an urbanised area, which meant mass casualties.

They passed a Chinese restaurant, a newsagent's, and a glass-fronted building society with half of its windows obliterated. Eventually, they made it onto the blockaded A411, empty aside from a few cars here or there that had crashed. The disaster must have distracted the drivers. They walked at a snail's pace, as if neither of them actually wanted to see what they were there to see. But there was no avoiding it, and around the very next bend in the road the devastation presented itself in its full, breathtaking plumage.

The wreckage no longer resembled a plane. It was more a piece of grotesque modern art. One white wing remained intact, jutting out of the supermarket's roof like it was still trying to cling to the sky, but the other wing was nowhere to be seen. Chunks of fuselage and simmering engine parts cluttered the supermarket's car park, along with masses of unidentifiable debris. Ashes and soot clung to every surface. All around, police struggled to console mortified onlookers and shell-shocked survivors. People screamed. Children cried. Husbands hugged their trembling wives. Mass tragedy was a tapestry Sarah could weave from memory, but each one had its own colour and smell. This one was subdued greys and blinding whites, with a sharp scent of burning chemicals.

Tragedy had once again struck the United Kingdom.

Once again, Sarah had to make sense of it.

The wreckage had been sectioned off by reams upon reams of police tape, making it impossible to get close. The only people within the inner cordon were rescue workers and firefighters dealing with several blazes still raging in and around the supermarket. Twisted blackened shopping trolleys scattered the crash site along with dozens of soot-covered vehicles. The windscreens of most had shattered.

Sergeant Mattock stood with a team two hundred metres away, easily recognisable from his combat uniform and the red bandana hanging from his breast pocket, which made it easier for his men to spot him in the field. When he saw Sarah and Thomas, he moved to greet them, grabbing Sarah by the arm and squeezing affectionately. "Good to see you, lass, but this is a shit show of epic proportions. Last I heard, there's seven hundred dead and more bodies being uncovered all the time. Not a single survivor from the plane and two-thirds of the people inside the supermarket copped it too. Someone will pay through the nose for this. This is the kind of fuck-up that bankrupts companies and puts even rich men in jail."

Thomas folded his arms and assumed an authoritative pose. "Is a malfunction suspected?"

Mattock shrugged. "I've been trying to get answers, but nobody is ready to share. There's a pair of crash scene investigators inside the cordon. I plan on grabbing one if I get the chance."

"Okay," said Thomas. "Good work, Sergeant. I'll check in with home base and find out where we're at. Let's hope this wasn't an intentional act."

They could all agree on that. The past few years had been relatively peaceful compared to the tumult of the preceding decade. The world had even started, dare Sarah think it, to feel safe. With Al-Sharir gone, the terrorism community had gone into hiding.

But there are always new madmen ready to take Al-Sharir's place.

Once Thomas was out of earshot, Mattock relaxed. He patted Sarah on the shoulder gently, which probably took concentration for a man more used to snapping necks. "How're things going with Howard's investigation? Ready to make a move yet?"

She shook her head. "Not yet, but the investigation is heating up. It won't be long before we pull the trigger."

He nodded over towards Thomas, who was on his phone twenty metres away. "You and him still doin' the merry dance?"

"Always. He still sees a future where he and I settle down and grow old together. I don't know if it's delusion or stubbornness. Anyway, right now I want to concentrate on what I'm looking at here. This is bad."

"Ain't it just." He moved closer to her and lowered his voice. "I didn't want to say it in front of our glorious leader, but there's a witness with a decent account of the crash. She's being treated for shock in the taxi rank across the road. You should go listen to what she has to say."

Sarah glanced in Thomas's direction and saw he was still busy on the phone. Across the road, several single-storey buildings had been battered by flaming debris, but a small taxi firm still had its windows intact. Parked outside it was an ambulance.

"Don't tell Thomas where I've gone," she said. "I'd like a chance to question her without an overseer."

"I thought you might. I'll tell him you went to take a shit."

Sarah chuckled, but she stopped herself when she saw the burning hellscape. Had she become so immune to such devastation that she could laugh?

If I didn't laugh, I would scream.

Sarah turned her back on the crash scene and crossed the empty, litter-strewn road. She headed around the ambulance and towards the taxi rank, where a bearded police officer greeted her at the entrance. She had to flash her badge to get by.

The taxi office was grimy and uncarpeted, with a tall reception desk taking up one side and a small leather sofa taking up the other. A middle-aged woman was sitting on the sofa with one arm stretched out across her knee while a paramedic took her blood pressure. A nasty scratch cleaved its way across the left side of her face and would likely leave a scar. Sarah could sympathise, although her disfigurement didn't bother her so much these days. Sometimes, she even used it to her advantage. During investigations, people either pitied her or were unsettled. Both reactions made it harder for people to lie to her.

Sarah flashed her badge at the paramedic and greeted the woman, who said her name was Eileen Chadwick. The poor dear was clearly in shock, alabaster-white and trembling like a drum skin. A stain on her thigh might have been from vomiting. "I'm really sorry to pester you, Eileen. My name is Sarah and I'm an agent with the MCU. I believe you witnessed today's accident."

Eileen gave a high-pitched squeak. "Accident? It was more than an accident. I thought the world was ending. I'll never forget it as long as I live."

The woman spoke loudly and energetically, which boded well. Shock was usually worse for the souls who turned sullen and unresponsive. Sarah nodded at the woman. "Of course, Eileen. It's an unbelievable tragedy, no question about it, but did you witness anything that might help make sense of what happened? Was the plane on fire when it came down? Any smoke coming from the engines?"

Eileen shook her head. "It fell out of the sky like a lump of coal. One second I was crossing the road, heading for the supermarket, the next, a plane comes down and explodes right in front of me. There was no fire or smoke. It just came down like a missile, nose pointed straight at the ground. It happened in a split second, but the image is imprinted on my brain."

Sarah raised an eyebrow. "It crashed straight into the ground? It didn't try to land or glide?"

"Nope. Was like a missile."

Sarah pointed to the scratch on Eileen's face. "Did that happen during the explosion?"

The woman acted as if she'd forgotten, hand rising towards her cheek, fingers prodding at the wound tentatively. "I... I think so. Never felt it at the time, but there was a lot of stuff flying through the air when the plane hit. I keep wondering..." She shook her head and let out a hollow chuckle. "I keep wondering what it was that hit my face. It could have been part of a person, you know? A piece of bone. A child's tooth."

"The debris was most likely from the plane's fuselage." Sarah didn't know if it was true, but she wanted to reassure the woman. It obviously failed because Eileen started hyperventilating. The paramedic gave Sarah a look that suggested she needed to go away. The last thing she wanted to do was harass a victim, so she thanked Eileen and left without complaint. She had learned a little, but not a lot.

Like a missile, she said.

Mattock stood where she'd left him. "She tell you the plane fell out of the sky like a dart?" he asked.

"Yeah. If it were a simple malfunction, the pilot would have tried to glide the plane down safely, right?"

"I've known pilots keep a plane in the air for an hour with no engines. Whatever this was, it was sudden. So sudden the pilot couldn't do a thing."

Thomas ended his phone call and rejoined them. "The pilot got off a twelve-second distress call before the plane crashed," he said. "The audio is with our analysts along with all the data from the cloud."

Sarah frowned. "The cloud?"

Mattock frowned as well. "What you talking about, boss?"

"Apparently, a handful of modern planes have been outfitted with the ability to send back flight data in real time. It's not as comprehensive as a black box, which we haven't discovered yet, but it'll give us the broad strokes of what happened. I'm going to head back to the earthworm and oversee the data gathering. Sarah, are you coming? You can brief your team and have them working on this. Take them off the Russian Mafia operation for now, okay?"

Sarah thought for a moment before deciding she didn't want to spend the next hour trapped in a car with Thomas. She needed to be active. She needed to be at this scene a while longer to let it fully sink into her bones. "No, I'm going to stick around here and try to get hold of the crash site investigators. I need to know more before I hand this off to my team."

Thomas looked put out, but he nodded. "Okay. I'll hang around another half hour and see what I can find out. Then I'll head off. You'll have to make your own way back."

"No problem, I'll get a taxi." Sarah looked back at the taxi firm's office being used as a treatment room. "Maybe one from the other side of town."

Thomas turned and put his phone back to his ear, but then he lowered it again and turned back. "Oh, did you find out anything from the witness?"

Sarah flinched. "Huh?"

Thomas chuckled. "All these years and you still hate having to work with others. I won't bother questioning the woman myself, but did you learn anything useful?"

It was true, Sarah hated having to rely on anybody else, but when she considered why she hadn't involved Thomas in the interview, it wasn't as simple as being antisocial. There were trust issues, to say the least, and working alone meant only having to trust herself. "I'm sorry. I should have had you join me, but I didn't learn anything anyway. Only that the plane was clearly out of control when it crashed. To be precise, the witness said it came down like a missile. Straight at the ground. Nose first."

Thomas winced. "That's not how planes come down. Not unless someone forces them."

"I know." Sarah nodded slowly. "My guts are telling me this was no accident. Somebody did this."

Mattock grunted. "Terrorism it is, then."

"Then we have work to do," said Thomas. "Let's go do it."

"I want y'all on this every second." Dr Jessica Bennett put her hands in the pockets of her lab coat, trying to hide their shaking.

"If you need to pee, grab a cup. If you need food, put your hand up and I'll get you a bag of chips. But do not stop working. Find me answers."

Jessica was in charge of the earthworm until Thomas returned. While the MCU was predominantly based in the UK, a sizeable chunk of its funding came from Washington, which was why both the director and deputy director were American. That was the trade-off agreed to by the Pentagon. Besides being American, however, there were few similarities between herself and Director Thomas Gellar.

Thomas was a schemer, always eyeing up whatever position was dangling directly overhead. There was a glint in his eye every time he met the prime minister or someone else high up in government. His regular updates to Pentagon officials were sickeningly self-aggrandising.

Jessica, on the other hand, cared about the MCU above all else. She had been a key component in its rebirth – along with Howard, Sarah, Mattock, and Palu. She and her colleagues had helped the agency to first survive, and then thrive. The Major Crimes Unit was their baby. Countless people were alive today because of its existence, and no matter what offers came her way, Jessica would forever dedicate herself to the continuing success of MCU. In fact, she had created her own promotion to deputy director rather than move somewhere else to further her career. She had fought for the position because she had feared Thomas's intentions for the agency after he had taken over from Palu, but she might possibly have overreacted. Despite Thomas's ruthless ambition, the MCU continued to do good work under Director Gellar's supervision.

I used to think Sarah was a train wreck, so perhaps I have a nasty habit of misjudgement.

Well, she pretty much is a train wreck, to be fair, but she's also the bravest son of a gun I ever met.

I should give Thomas a break.

"Ma'am?"

Jessica glanced at one of her analysts. The team was spread in a circle, analysts sitting at computers spaced around the room's perimeter. Jessica stood in the centre, overseeing a bunch of stuff she barely understood. The analyst was named Manraj. He was just a kid – or at least it felt that way to her – but he was bright and motivated. "What is it, Raj?"

"I downloaded the pilot's mayday recording from air traffic control."

"Okay, great. Play it for me."

Manraj turned up the volume on his monitor and double-clicked a file on his desktop. A congested audio recording started playing, a pair of panicked male voices amidst a cacophony of beeping alarms and howling wind. "*...out of control... systems not responding... interference... losing altitude. Help...*" A pause. "*I can't...*" Silence.

The audio didn't end with an explosion. It just cut off.

"Is that all we have?"

Manraj was half swivelled around in his seat. Her lack of enthusiasm deflated him. "We're receiving flight telemetry from the Civil Aviation Authority," he said positively. "That should tell us the condition of the plane when it came down. If the health monitors were working as they should have been, we can try to narrow down what malfunctioned – or find out which parts of the plane were overridden."

"Overridden?"

Manraj shrugged. "Well, yes, it's a possibility. The pilot made no mention of anyone physically threatening the plane, but if this was a malicious act, it could have been a cyberattack."

Jessica pinched her nose behind her spectacles and took a deep breath. "Are you telling me criminals can hack into planes and fly them into the ground now? Is that where we're at?"

"It hasn't happened yet" – Manraj sounded unsure – "and it probably hasn't happened now, but in theory it could be possible. The more advanced aircraft become, the more they rely on automated systems and complex software. All software can be hacked if a person understands it well enough. I actually studied the potential risk of cyberattacks against airliners as part of my final year dissertation. I think it's possible that—"

"Okay, Manraj. Let's just focus on the evidence in front of us, okay? Don't get ahead of yourself."

A chill slithered down Jessica's spine. Manraj was clearly projecting his biases onto the investigation, which was a sign of his inexperience, but there was, of course, the chance he might be correct. Youth brought new ideas, and new ideas were right as often as they were wrong.

Why hijack a plane and commit suicide when you can just hack into one from a laptop and watch the fireworks show?

Terrorism had only grown more frightening as the years passed by. The bad guys weren't KGB spies or lone gunmen any more. The threats were both invisible and in plain sight. Hackers, viruses, school shooters… Heck, there were even economic terrorists to contend with nowadays – financial wizards who could destabilise a country's financial well-being by manipulating the markets. The number and types of threats had multiplied and were even more indiscriminate in their targeting. The entry conditions for terrorism had lowered substantially, and in these heady days of 2021, a dingy call centre in India could steal more money from the local economy than ten teams of bank robbers – and to make matters worse, the scammers usually got away with it. Crime was starting to pay, and there were better ways to skin a cat than homemade bombs and rusty AK47s. Terrorism had got smarter, more efficient.

And I'm losing my understanding of it. This room is full of postgrads with more knowledge of today's threats than I have after twelve years at the MCU. How can I lead them when I don't understand what it is they're doing?

I'm forty-four and already too old for this.

Jessica stood in the centre of the room for what might have been half an hour, so lost in thought that she flinched when an analyst called out to her. "Dr Bennett?"

Jessica turned to face a junior analyst with short blonde hair and purple lipstick. "Yes, Carrie? What do you have?"

"I've found something that doesn't make a lot of sense."

Jessica peered over Carrie's shoulder at her monitor. All she saw were lines of white code against a black background, as well as a pair of graphs in a separate window. "What am I looking at?"

"It's the plane's firewall. It recorded a possible hacking attempt before the flight crashed. That's not unusual – planes have been under threat from hacktivists and criminals for several years now – but the worst that usually happens is that the plane's Wi-Fi or infotainment system gets exploited. A hacker might spy on an influential passenger's emails or download the pictures from a person's phone, but little else."

Jessica nodded, understanding so far. "Okay. So what about the plane's mechanical systems? Could somebody hack into those?"

"It shouldn't be possible. At least, not if my understanding is correct. The aircraft's systems are segmented. The mechanical controls can't accept remote commands. Only... I found corrupted code in both the plane's autopilot systems and the altimeter readings. From what I can see, the aircraft thought it was flying straight, but it was actually flying towards the ground. The altered code was less than a hundred characters. That's all it took."

Jessica's stomach churned. She imagined the panic onboard when the plane suddenly turned vertical and started hurtling towards the ground. She heard the passenger's screams, their desperate pleas. She pictured terrified parents clutching their bewildered children. "You just said an aircraft's mechanical systems can't be hacked."

Carrie nodded but appeared flummoxed. "They can't. Except that's what happened. I've traced a signature in the firewall recordings to an android device. The connection was made via Bluetooth."

"Android? You're telling me the corrupt code came from a mobile phone or a tablet?"

"Yes, ma'am. From inside the plane. Bluetooth has a very limited range, you see, so—"

Jessica groaned and waved a hand. "I get it, Carrie. You're saying this might have been a suicide bomber?"

Carried nodded, her face growing pale. "One of the passengers crashed the plane."

Sarah stood, watching a girl no older than six weep into her father's arms. According to one of the paramedics, they had been waiting in the supermarket car park while the mother had gone inside to grab a chicken for dinner. She never made it out.

If planes were going to start falling out of the sky, then the world was about to change for the worse, like it had after 9/11. Technology was an indiscriminate weapon that developed faster than the people using it, and the fact that it was nearly twenty years since the Twin Towers fell was an eerie coincidence.

Is this an anniversary attack?

Thomas finished his latest phone call and approached Sarah. He offered a grim smile and asked if she was sure she didn't want to head back to the earthworm with him. She took another look at the young girl and distraught father and declined. "This is where I need to be right now. I need to feel it."

Thomas frowned but didn't argue. His cheeks were grey and sagging, tiredness taking its toll. "Call me with any updates, okay? Where's Mattock?"

"Trying to get some airtime with the crash investigators. Did you learn anything over the phone?"

"Not much. Jessica has the hive working on the flight data, but from what I gather, the plane might have been using new technology. The analysts aren't fully up to speed on it."

Sarah groaned. "Let me guess. This new technology is supposed to make a plane safer?"

"I don't know, but whatever the cause of the crash, it's going to be a long day."

"Yeah, no kidding. I'll call you if anything turns up, okay? Do the same for me?"

"Of course." He put his hand on her shoulder and smiled wearily. Then he left.

The February afternoon was chilly. The sky had darkened with the promise of night, and by five o'clock the weak sun would be gone. Harsh floodlights would then be brought in to light the scene. Right now, the site was swarming with news vans and yapping journalists, but no helicopters flew overhead, suggesting the local airspace had been closed – or maybe even the national airspace. That was likely Thomas's doing. Sarah didn't always agree with him, but she had to admit he was proactive and led from the front. He didn't wait around for answers to come to him, he went after them himself. She had always liked that about him.

Sarah intended to search for Mattock, but someone grabbed her from behind, hard enough to make her twist and shrug them off. "What the hell are you—"

The journalist was familiar, a woman in her forties often seen reporting from the doorsteps of Downing Street or outside Parliament. "Hello," she yapped. "I'm Kate Amy with Cloud News. You're Ms Stone, senior supervisor with the MCU, correct?"

Sarah rolled her eyes. "I suppose my face gives me away, huh? What are you doing inside the cordon, Amy?"

A microphone prodded at Sarah's chin. A camera pointed at her from a few feet away. "Early reports suggest this may have been an act of cyberterrorism. Can you confirm or deny this, please?"

How the hell does she know?

"Go away."

The microphone jabbed at her again, nearly hitting her face.

"Please, our viewers want to understand what caused today's tragedy. They have a right to know."

"Who did you pay for this little ambush, sweetheart? One of the plods at the cordon, or someone higher up? Either way, you're intruding on a tragedy and my attempts to make sense of it."

"Ms Stone, please answer my question. Was Flight CAS8-96 brought down by an act of terrorism?"

How about I bring you down, you meddling bitch?

"I suggest you step away before that microphone ends up somewhere unpleasant."

"What is the MCU doing about this disaster? Has the agency failed to protect the United Kingdom once again, as it did with Wazir Hesbani and Al Al-Sharir? Or when your father, Major Stone, attacked Parliament?"

Sarah had put in a lot of work controlling her temper in recent years, but she had a special disliking for journalists. Before she knew it, she was lashing out, swinging her leg and planting a boot right on the other woman's kneecap. Senior reporter Kate Amy dropped like a sack of spuds, squealing in agony. The cameraman gasped, but he didn't move to help her. Instead, he pointed the camera at her pain-wracked face.

"She assaulted me. She assaulted me. Help."

Sarah shrugged. "See you in court."

Damn it, Sarah.

The last thing she needed was to get swallowed up in a load of drama. The nearby police officers might try to arrest her if they got wind of an assault.

Or they can try at least.

The reporter's screaming was drawing a crowd, so Sarah got moving, heading closer to the smouldering plane crash. She found Mattock at the edge of the supermarket's car park and positioned herself behind him. He was briefing a pair of field agents, but he dismissed them when he saw her.

"I just assaulted a journalist," she said.

He chuckled. "You've really got to stop doing that, lass."

"Well, at least my boss won't fire me. You find out anything?"

Mattock gave a shrug and rubbed at the greying stubble on his chin. He looked older than the last time she'd seen him, which had only been a couple of months ago. "Not a thing," he admitted. "The crash investigators are a prickly pair. They won't say a word until their findings are complete. Worried about saying the wrong thing, I suppose. Can't blame 'em, really. The higher-ups will want to control the narrative."

"Mattock, if this plane really was hacked, the aerospace industry is finished. We'll be back to travelling by boat by the end of the week. The investigators didn't give you any kind of hint?"

"No, but they did let slip that it was unlikely someone on the ground could have done this. There's a first time for everything, though, aye?" He tilted his head towards the commotion at the edge of the cordon, where Kate Amy was currently feigning near-death. No doubt she was weaving tales of brutality for the two police officers trying to help her. "How did the sodding press get privileges so quickly?"

"Someone got paid, obviously. If I find out who, I'll—" Her phone buzzed in her thigh pocket. She pulled the Velcro strap and lifted the flap. The ringtone, once again, alerted her to who it was. "Jessica? I'm on the ground. It's bad. Real bad. Please, tell me you have something."

"Sarah, that gosh-darned plane was hacked. It's supposed to be impossible, but Flight CAS8-96 was testing out a new anti-terrorism protocol."

"You're telling me this new anti-terrorism protocol allowed the plane to get hijacked remotely?"

"That's about the colour of it, Sarah. They outfitted the pilot with a prototype app on his phone, allowing him to transfer the aircraft's flight controls over to the tower in the event of a hijacking. From how it's been explained to me, it means that if the pilot gets locked out of the cockpit or kept from the controls, one button press on his mobile phone can take control of the airplane away from the hijackers and pass it to ground control, who can land it safely via a future assisted-landing system."

"And this new safety measure allowed someone to hack into the plane?"

"Yes and no."

Sarah sighed. "What does that mean, Jess?"

"It means that hacking directly into the plane still wasn't possible. The only device capable of remote access was the pilot's phone. It was synced with the plane before take-off."

"So the pilot brought down the plane? Jesus."

"No, that's not what I'm saying, Sarah. Someone hacked into the pilot's phone and used it to transfer the control protocol to themselves."

"That sounds... complicated." Sarah swallowed a lump in her throat, trying to understand what she was hearing. Mattock was staring at her, looking even more confused.

Jessica took a breath and continued. "Sometimes, I think this latest bunch of analysts are speaking a different language, but as I understand it, this was a hack on top of a hack. The pilot's phone was a backdoor into the plane's flight controls and someone took advantage of that. Whoever designed the new security protocol spent far too long worrying about someone trying to seize the plane directly and not enough time thinking about someone seizing the one device that could actually take control."

Sarah clawed at the tight blonde ponytail at the back of her head, wanting to tear out her hair. "So, the hacker downloaded the pilot's dick pics, made a few prank calls, then crashed the plane into the ground? We need to catch this psycho before he does it again. It's been twenty years since 9/11, Jess. This could be the start of something."

"Don't you think I know that? I lost family in New York. Twenty years might sound like a long time, but it's not."

Sarah sighed. "You lost a cousin, right?"

"Sweet little Veronica. Hair the colour of fresh straw and a smile that could light up a coal mine. Anyway, I have an address for you. You want it?"

"What? You have a lead on a suspect?"

"As good as the hacker was, the hive got an IP address. Fancy paying a house call?"

Sarah looked towards the cordon, at the distraught father and his motherless little girl. "I'm already on my way."

CHAPTER FOUR

Cosmo was a reliable soldier, but sometimes he struggled to get to the point. That was a problem for Maxim because time was money. He growled and prodded a thick, gold-ringed index finger in Cosmo's face. "Get to the point, Cousin. What interest is this plane crash to me?"

Cosmo was a hardened killer from Novokuznetsk, but he flinched at Maxim's rising anger. He took off his blue baseball cap and clutched it by his waist. "I am telling you that our good friend, Ivan Zakharov, is dead. He was aboard plane that crash in Watford this afternoon. I am sorry to bring such news."

Maxim's eyes widened. Although he had never shed a tear for anyone, he felt the merest pang of sadness in his heart. "Ivan is dead? He was like brother to me. We serve as police officers in Orsk. The times we have – *ha!* – would have made Devil himself blush." He placed a hand over his breast. "Ivan, you were a true Cossack. Rest in peace, my friend."

Cosmo did the sign of the cross. He didn't leave, which meant he obviously had more to say. Maxim told him to spit it out. "Yes, boss. It is strange thing. Our asset in Metropolitan Police say it might be hacker who bring down plane."

Maxim wasn't sure he heard correctly. "Say that again, Cousin."

"Details come through. They say hacker take control of plane and crash. From ground."

Maxim folded his arms and leant back against the wall. They were standing inside the office at the back of the garage, so they were alone. His Colt Python knocked against his ribs beneath his coat. "Such a thing would take a great deal of skill, no? Any idea who might have been behind such a thing? Our friends in Moscow, perhaps?"

"I do not know this, but MCU is leading criminal side of investigation." Cosmo smirked, knowing what that meant. "It is good thing we have friends in high places, no?"

Maxim put a hand on the back of Cosmo's neck and bumped their heads together. "*Za uspekh*, my cousin."

Cosmo left the office and got inside an old orange BMW M3 parked over the mechanic's pit. Its boot was full of guns, but its registration belonged to an eighty-year-old woman in a coma, courtesy of a friend working in the country's palliative care services.

Cosmo had been a teenager dealing drugs for a local kingpin when Maxim had found him. He tried to steal Maxim's Mercedes SL350 while he was getting coffee, but surrendered when Maxim tapped a Makarov against the driver's side window. After breaking the boy's arm, Maxim decided to help Cosmo by taking care of the local kingpin. The short skirmish with a thirty-year-old Iranian with gold teeth and tattoos ended quickly via a shotgun blast to the face. Maxim had carved an inked image of the Virgin Mary from his dead enemy's shoulder and kept it as a memento. It was still preserved inside a lockbox he kept, full of various reminders of his glorious and bloody history.

Maxim sat down on his office chair and crossed one leg over the other, causing his trousers to ride up to the top of his argyle socks. After a moment's thought, he pulled out his phone and made a call. "Thomas? You must be very busy, but what is this I hear about hacker with magical power to bring down planes?"

Thomas sighed down the phone. "Nothing's been confirmed yet. It's only speculation."

"Speculation is prelude to truth, no? If hacker bring down plane, I want to meet this man. You will make sure I get chance, before anyone does something silly like try to arrest."

"There's no way," said Thomas forcefully. "If an individual caused what happened today, they'll be the most wanted criminal on the planet. I won't let you get involved in this. This is bigger than you."

"Thomas, I am asking for simple favour. If you find this genius, you tell me moment you find out, yes? All I need is name and address. I take care of rest. You and me, Thomas, we help one another, no? Why change what has worked so well? I would hate to see our friendship dissolve like limbs in barrel full of acid."

Thomas grunted, probably sneering down the phone at Maxim. He clearly understood the threat, for he was no idiot, but he had grown insolent lately. Maxim could ruin Thomas Gellar in a thousand different ways, but the cleanest option would be to make him disappear. "If I learn anything, I'll let you know, but don't bank on it."

Maxim chuckled, but it was a deadly sound, perfected by years of menacing proud men. "I will not be disappointed, Thomas. You can bank on *that*."

Maxim ended the call, knowing his message would be received. Like all Americans, Thomas detested being subservient, but he lacked the spine to disobey. Only men with principles disobeyed, and the head of the MCU had none besides self-preservation.

A man with power to crash planes would be very useful to my enterprise. My enemies travel by air. My allies too.

I have new job opening.

. . .

Oliver had arrived at work twenty minutes ago. He'd been sitting alone for the last ten. His boss, Mr Stewart, liked to leave early on a Saturday, and today he had been in a particular hurry. There must have been a big match on at the pub.

The computer repair shop got busier over the weekends, but never so much that one person couldn't handle things by themselves. Being alone was fine with Ollie because he needed to think. He needed to think about what he'd done, and about what might happen next. If he'd covered his tracks as well as he'd hoped, things might be okay, but if he'd left even the slightest of breadcrumbs, then law enforcement would track him down. In that case, his biggest hope was that it would take them a while. Maybe he would have time to flee the country and go into hiding.

I'm seventeen years old and have a part-time job at a computer repair shop. How am I going to flee the country? I'm screwed. It doesn't matter if it was an accident.

I killed people.

Oliver had been avoiding it for the last twenty minutes, but he finally gathered his courage enough to move the mouse attached to the computer at the front desk. With the operating system installed on an SSD, the screen fizzed to life immediately. The checkout software started, but Oliver minimised it and double-clicked the browser icon. As was probably the case for two-thirds of the globe, Google loaded. Oliver didn't know what to search, so after a moment's hesitation, he simply settled on the word 'News'.

A quarter of the way down the page, a row of images featured a horrific plane crash. Oliver hadn't even known where the plane had landed until he clicked on the first link and brought up an article from the *Times*.

700 people confirmed dead in Watford.

. . .

I killed seven hundred people.

Oliver lurched forward over the desk and vomited. His stomach was empty, but the entire pint of water he'd drunk when he'd arrived at work flooded the floor on the customer side of the desk. He tried to get up off his stool but collapsed onto the floor and vomited again – acid and bile. His stomach continued to purge itself until his seizing diaphragm put a stop to it. He lay there on the floor, moaning miserably.

This morning, he'd been screwing around on his computer as normal, hacking into air traffic control to see how deep he could get before the firewall booted him out. It was a game, one he had started when flight simulators and dogfighting games had ceased providing enough in the way of thrills. The enjoyment came from the challenge, in seeing how deep he could get. At first, he had hacked lightly secured feeds – chatter between pilots and radio towers – but then he had learned how to hack into airline passenger manifests and stored payment details. Recently, he had even hacked individual planes, breaking into their onboard Wi-Fi and accessing the personal devices connected to it. The thrill he got, downloading passenger's raunchy pictures, private emails, and account passwords, was awesome, and he barely believed he was doing it, but when the fun ended, he disposed of everything. He was no criminal. He didn't steal or blackmail. The game was never about hurting anybody. It was only about proving he could do it.

Then, at eleven this morning, he had gone deeper than ever before. He hacked into a plane's Wi-Fi, as he had done a dozen times by now, and then broke into a random android device connected to that Wi-Fi. The device obviously belonged to the pilot, because many of the images in the camera roll were of planes, cockpits, and various flight crews. Aside from wanting to be the world's best hacker, Oliver often dreamt of becoming a pilot, so the man's private life intrigued him enough to keep digging. The last thing he did – before the Wi-Fi went dead and air traffic control started panicking over the airwaves – was brute-force his way into an app that he didn't recognise. It had a high level of protection, which had only made him more determined.

Then the plane had crashed.

Somehow, an application on the pilot's phone had brought down the plane.

Because I messed with it. Because I messed with something I shouldn't have.

The bell above the front door jingled. A customer stepped inside.

"We're closed," Oliver moaned, still lying on the floor beside a pool of his own stomach acids. "I can't help you!"

And nobody can help me.

The address Jessica had provided led Sarah and Mattock to an average middle-class housing estate in the town of Ipswich. The tedious drive left Sarah's body tingling with a desire for action, but when they arrived, their destination felt wrong. If someone had asked earlier where one might expect to find a cyberterrorist's lair, Sarah would've pictured an abandoned factory or a secret set-up in the backroom of a dingy shop. She most definitely would not have pictured a semi-detached house in a leafy suburb.

Mattock positioned the Range Rover across the property's short driveway, blocking a nearly new Volkswagen Touareg parked in front of a single garage. He put a call through to Thomas and updated him on their location, but Sarah got out and peered through the Volkswagen's tinted rear windows, hoping to see a boot full of sophisticated electronics. Unfortunately, it was impossible to make out anything besides vague shapes.

Mattock joined her on the driveway a minute later, a frown upon his face. "Nice gaff, aye?"

"You sure this is the right address?" There was a cute little cement turtle in the front garden with daffodils growing out of a hole in its shell. "I'm not getting alarm bells."

"Trust in thy satnav, lass. This is the address Bennett gave us."

Mattock knocked on the front door – a piece of white moulded PVC with a stained glass panel at the top. Its brass handle was badly burnished. A shadow appeared behind the glass panel a few seconds later and the door opened. A woman in her early fifties appeared, hair tied back in a high ponytail and skin gleaming with moisturiser. She was wearing pyjamas, but that didn't seem to embarrass her. She appeared startled to see them, which was a fair enough reaction considering Sarah's grizzly scars and Mattock's grizzly *everything*.

"Um, hello? Can I help you both?"

"Yes, good afternoon, ma'am," said Sarah. "We're with the MCU. Agents Stone and Mattock. Is this the Simpson residence?"

"Yes, I'm Mrs Simpson. What on earth do you want?"

"Do you use a computer at this address?"

Mrs Simpson frowned. "Of course I do. Who doesn't use a computer?"

"Good point. Can we come inside for a moment? We'd like to talk to you about a delicate matter."

"Well, I'm not sure about that. Do you have any ID? You look like a pair of bailiffs."

Mattock chuckled, and he peeled the badge from the breast pocket of his shirt that also held his red bandana. His entire uniform was made up of pockets, but at least he had left his weapons and rigging inside the lockbox beneath the Range Rover's boot shelf. "Sorry about our appearances," he said, holding up his ID, "but I promise our manners are better than our looks."

Mrs Simpson gave a subtle smile, charmed by Mattock's gruff yet friendly accent. "I suppose you'd better come in then. I was about to get dressed and rush out to the gym, so make it quick."

Sarah nodded. "Of course, ma'am. We'll clear things right up."

They entered the hallway, which was immaculately tidy, with a posh anthracite shield over the radiator and a bejewelled mirror above. The floor was some kind of wood-effect vinyl, clunky under foot and possibly in need of relaying.

Mrs Simpson led them into a modest country-style kitchen and then pointed to an adjoining dining room. "Take a seat."

Sarah thanked her, and she and Mattock sat down on cream chairs arranged around a circular table with a vase full of fake purple flowers in the centre.

Mrs Simpson remained standing in the doorway, arms folded, posture guarded. "Now, what exactly does the MCU want with me? You're the terrorist people, right?"

Sarah clasped her hands together on the table and nodded. "We're here because our cybersecurity team flagged this address in a recent investigation. Do you know why that might be?"

"I have utterly no idea. Cybersecurity? Are you talking about illegal downloads or something?" She raised her hands in the air. "I admit it. I've downloaded the odd dodgy film in the past, but it was never worth it. *The Greatest Showman* filmed on a mobile phone isn't so great." Sarah and Mattock frowned and remained silent. Mrs Simpson put her hands down and tutted. "I'm joking. Look, whatever you're investigating has nothing to do with me. My husband and I own a chip shop in town. We sell saveloys for a living. You have the wrong house."

"Love me a saveloy," said Mattock, licking his lips.

"Well, drop by some time. They're on me. Now, can I get going, please? This is a little ridiculous, to tell you the truth."

"Mrs Simpson..." Sarah chose to be blunt. "Our investigators have connected this address to a recent cybercrime. I'm talking about hacking, breaking into secure systems, that kind of thing."

Mrs Simpson snorted and covered her mouth. "You're off

your trolley. I can barely open my emails. Ha! You must be having me on. Is this a joke?"

Sarah had dealt with domestic terrorists before – the Fosters being the ones who came to mind – but Ms Simpson was displaying no obvious signs of duplicity. In fact, she appeared genuinely nonplussed. You could never tell for sure, but the woman seemed genuine.

Jessica wouldn't have passed on bad intel. If the hive flagged this address, it's for a reason.

"Mrs Simpson..."

"Rebecca, please. You're making me feel old."

"Rebecca. You said you and your husband live here. Can we speak with him?"

"He's gone out to play snooker with a friend before work, but he's no more technical than I am. Our son calls us a couple of cavemen."

Sarah leant forward, knocking the table with her elbow and causing the vase of fake flowers to wobble. "You have a son? Does he live here with you?"

"Well, yes, but I assure you that Ollie has done nothing wrong. He's never so much as shoplifted."

"Is he here now?" asked Mattock, sitting straight and craning his neck towards the kitchen.

"No, he's at work. But I told you, he's done nothing."

Sarah raised an eyebrow at the woman. "Does he use a computer?"

"Of course he uses a computer – he's seventeen. He's glued to screens like every other teenager."

Sarah stood up and stepped away from the table. "Do you mind if we look at his computer, Rebecca?"

Mrs Simpson unfolded her arms. "Now, see here. I won't allow you to come inside my home and start invading my son's privacy. What is really going on here? I'm getting annoyed."

Sarah sighed. A mother's ferocity knew no bounds, so it would be unwise to play hardball. She chose her words carefully.

"For whatever reason, our investigation has led us here, Rebecca, and the matter won't go away unless you cooperate with us. If your son is innocent, as you say, then his computer will prove that. If this is a false alarm, we would sooner deal with it quickly and move on."

"I'm not comfortable with this." She shook her head. "People get all kinds of things on their computers without knowing it. I'm not having you arrest Ollie over something silly like... like..." She covered her mouth. Her hand trembled. "Please, tell me this isn't about porn. Are you saying Ollie downloaded something horrible? I think... I think I need you to leave. You're not going to—"

Sarah put a hand up. "Rebecca? I can't go into detail about what we're looking for, but I will say, categorically, that we are not looking for indecent images. This is something else. And quite frankly, I'm hoping we do indeed have the wrong address. If you don't let us check Ollie's computer, we'll be back with a dozen police officers and a warrant. That might sound like blackmail, but it's a simple fact. Work with us here, Rebecca, and if your son has done nothing wrong, we'll be out of your hair right away. You have my word."

Mrs Simpson looked close to tears. No mother wanted to suspect their child of wrongdoing, but in this day and age it was easy to live a secret life. Teenagers could get into all kinds of trouble without their parents suspecting a thing. Right now, Mrs Simpson was probably imagining a hundred devastating scenarios.

"Ollie's bedroom is the first at the top of the stairs." She swallowed loudly and licked her lips. "I'll wait here."

Mattock stood up and put a hand on Mrs Simpson's elbow. "Make yourself a cuppa, love. Hopefully, we'll be gone by the time you finish it."

Sarah started up the stairs in the hallway. A large window spilled weak sunlight over the bend, and a magpie flew past outside. It reminded her of the downed plane in Watford and the hundreds who had died onboard. This really didn't feel like the home of a mass murderer. It was a little too neat, and at the same time slightly dilapidated, but aside from that, it was a warm, welcoming place.

As Mrs Simpson had said, Ollie's bedroom was the first at the top of the stairs. It was a typical lad's room, with superhero posters on the wall and an unmade single bed. Shelves on the wall held *Star Wars* toys and other colourful knick-knacks. A desk in the corner played host to a mess of wires, hardware, and a large wraparound monitor.

"That looks like a pretty expensive rig to me," said Mattock, pointing to an oversized PC tower underneath the desk. The side panel was made of glass, displaying a maze of cables and components within. The unit was currently switched off, which caused Sarah to speculate. Wouldn't someone seriously into their tech prefer a computer to go to sleep than to switch off? Give the mouse a nudge and you're back in business, no waiting around. Just to be sure, she nudged the mouse to see if it brought anything to life. It didn't.

Did Ollie switch the computer off in a panic? Did he fear being traced?

She pressed the computer's power button, a silver disc on top of the case, and the fans whirred. The system booted quickly and quietly. The monitor came out of standby and displayed a crisp login screen. Sarah lacked the skills to break into the computer, but she noticed something of interest without having to. Although the background image was blurred by the login overlay, it was obvious what it was – a fuzzy grid of green text against a black backdrop like a scene from *The Matrix*. It was the type of thing a hacker might conceivably choose for desktop wallpaper. It was nowhere near evidential, but Sarah's doubts about this being the wrong address began to evaporate.

"You think this is our kid?" asked Mattock. He was shaking his head and grimacing. "Shit, could it really *be* a kid?"

"I don't know," said Sarah, "but kids today know more about

computers than we can even fathom. We need to get a team working on this PC. We won't know anything until—"

Sarah froze.

Mattock frowned. "What's wrong, lass?"

She nodded past him to a small side table at the foot of the room's single bed. Several toys took up space on it, but only one of them interested her. The die-cast passenger plane was perched on a slender stand, pointing towards the sky. "Ollie has a fondness for airplanes," she said. "Or maybe a love of watching them fall out of the sky."

Mattock swore under his breath. "We need to bring this kid in, don't we?"

"Yes."

Mrs Simpson clearly hadn't wanted to give up her son's location, but when Sarah had faked putting out an alert for Oliver's immediate arrest, the mother finally complied. The address she gave was yet another red flag – Oliver Simpson worked part-time at a computer repair shop. Based on that, and the custom-built rig in his bedroom, the kid was clearly tech savvy. The question was, *how* tech savvy?

Sarah had a bad feeling.

Could a kid really have done this?

The computer repair shop was less than two miles away, so it took no time at all to reach it. Despite the brief journey, Thomas had been on the radio twice, wanting to know her every move and sounding stressed. That was understandable, considering his position. It was his arse on the line if they failed to catch whoever was behind today's tragedy. It was the worst single-cause death toll in the UK's peacetime history.

Mattock parked the Range Rover in a parallel bay at the side of the road, directly in front of the computer shop. The window was plastered with posters for upgrades, repairs, and component sales, which made it next to impossible to see inside, but from first inspections, it appeared to be a legitimate business.

Sarah exited the Range Rover and stepped out onto the pavement. She glanced up and felt a slight drizzle against the unscarred side of her face. There was electricity in the air, the promise of a storm.

Mattock got out and locked the car. "We going in easy? Or should I arm up?"

"I have my Sig, but let's leave the big toys in the boot. Don't want to frighten anybody unnecessarily, do we. It's just a kid and we're in a built-up area."

"You're the boss."

It wasn't true, as she and Mattock shared equal rank, but she appreciated his faith in her. More and more, Mattock had become like a kindly uncle, always watching over her but never interfering.

Sarah pushed on the glass and aluminium door and entered the shop. Her boots came down on a spongy laminate floor, and a bell jingled overhead, heralding her arrival. Variously sized plastic packets hung from pegs on the wall and colourful boxes perched on shelves. A single desk occupied the shop floor, but no one stood behind it. A subtle miasma of vomit and citrus hung in the air without a visible cause.

Did someone chuck their guts up in here?

"Hello?" Mattock searched left and right. "Service?"

A young man appeared from an open doorway behind the desk dressed in a white shirt and black trousers. He was pale, with puffy eyes that made it appear as if he'd been crying. His floppy blonde hair needed a wash. When he saw them standing on the shop floor, he froze.

"H-Hi there. What can I help you with?"

"Need a printer cable," said Mattock nonchalantly. Sarah immediately understood what he was doing. If they asked to speak with an Oliver Simpson, the kid might bolt out the rear exit or even grab a weapon. Better to progress things cautiously.

The young man visibly relaxed. He stepped out from behind the desk and pointed. "Oh, yes. I can get you one of those. What you need is an A-to-B USB cable, most likely. We have them over here." He walked to the left-hand side of the shop. Sarah instinctively moved towards the desk, making sure she was closer to the rear exit than he was.

Mattock smiled amiably, which was miraculous considering the tapestry of scars crisscrossing his shaven skull. "What's your name, lad? Feel like I know you from somewhere. Tom, right?"

"No. No, my name's Oliver."

"Ollie, for short, I'd bet?"

The kid nodded. He was jittery, like he'd drunk too much coffee – or was nervous about something. "Y-You don't sound like you're from around here, sir."

"Manchester born and bred. I'm a travelling salesman, and I've gone and left me printer cable at home, ain't I? Bloody forget me head, I would."

Oliver chuckled and relaxed further. "Think you're supposed to say 'salesperson' these days, and you don't much look like one."

Mattock ran a hand over his scarred dome. "Past life as a cage fighter. I were doing it long before it became fashionable."

"I'm not really into MMA. Too violent."

"It is that."

Over by the desk, Sarah was now certain she smelled vomit and an accompanying odour of bleach. She tried to peek into the backroom but saw nothing besides a long desk full of lifeless computers and scattered tools.

Oliver reached up and plucked a plastic packet from a peg. "Here's what you need, sir. Is there anything else?"

"Yeah," said Mattock, and he flashed his MCU badge. "Something terrible happened today, lad, and I reckon you might know something about it."

"What?" Oliver stepped back just as Mattock attempted to grab him. The kid glanced towards the rear exit, but Sarah stepped in his way and erased any hope of making a run for it. Mattock blocked the front entrance. They had him trapped. That Oliver Simpson had even considered fleeing made it unlikely they had the wrong person.

Mattock switched on a menacing scowl. Sarah played good cop. "Ollie? We have questions we need to ask. Please, don't panic, okay? We're not here to hurt you."

The kid teetered back and forth. He'd turned deathly pale. "I... I didn't mean it. It was an accident."

Sarah's insides twisted.

So he did do it.

This nervous young man had killed seven hundred people. A mass murderer history would never forget.

But he's terrified.

Sarah put up both hands, showing she was unarmed. Beneath her jacket, her Sig hid in its modified holster below her left armpit. "We just want to find out what happened today, Ollie."

"I don't know. Really, I don't."

"Are you trying to say it wasn't you?" said Mattock. He took a half step and sneered. "We're talking about hundreds of innocent people dying helplessly. Women. Children. That was you, wasn't it? Don't lie to me, boy."

Oliver opened his mouth to speak, but no words came out. Tears swelled in his eyes. He appeared ready to collapse, but instead he bolted. There was nowhere for him to go, but the unexpected move gave him a split-second advantage. He rushed over to one of the product displays and grabbed something from a peg – a large screwdriver with a big rubber grip. He held it out in his shaking hands, the manufacturer's label dangling from a hole in the handle. "L-Leave me alone. Just... leave me alone."

Sarah whipped out her Sig and pointed it at the kid's chest. It was the last thing she wanted to do, but she reminded herself what the kid had done. Seven hundred victims demanded she take him in. "You're going to need something better than a screwdriver, Ollie, because I have a gun with twelve bullets. You can come with us willingly or with a bullet in your kneecap. Your choice, but I'm sure your mum would prefer me not to shoot you."

He flinched. "Y-You spoke to my mum?"

"Of course. She's worried about you."

Oliver shook his head and started whimpering. "Get out, get out, get out!"

"Quit yer bawlin'." Mattock lunged at the kid, causing him to flinch and lash out with the screwdriver. His attack missed, but Sarah glanced at Mattock and motioned for him to step back. Oliver was panicking, but if they calmed him down, he might see sense and come with them. He was clearly hysterical, not a cold-blooded psychopath.

Unless he's one hell of an actor.

Sarah lowered her Sig and pointed it at the cheap laminate flooring. "Oliver, listen to me, okay? My name's Sarah. I understand today is a very bad day for you, but it's going to get much worse if you don't settle down and come with us. We're the good guys, okay?"

"You don't look like good guys. What happened to your face?"

"You have bigger things to worry about than my scars. You need to think about yourself right now. There's an opportunity for you to cooperate and explain your side of things, but the window is closing."

"I... I..."

"You're scared – I get it – but you're under eighteen, which means your mum and dad will be with you every step of the way. You won't be alone. Put down the screwdriver, okay? It's the only way this can play out. I don't want to have to shoot you."

The kid kept the screwdriver pointed at Mattock and sobbed fiercely. The torment on his face was hard to witness. "I don't want to go to prison," he said. "I want my mum."

Sarah nodded. "We'll get her, okay? But you have to put down the screwdriver."

He looked her in the eye, his hysteria subsiding for a moment. "I'm in so much trouble, aren't I?"

Sarah hated to do it, but she nodded. "Yeah, kid. I won't lie to you, it's going to be bad, but no one is going to hurt you. I promise."

Oliver placed the screwdriver against his throat. "I don't want to be here."

Sarah gave Mattock the nod. "Move!"

Mattock grabbed Oliver's arm before the kid could hurt himself. He was twice the size, so it was easy for him to take control, and within three seconds Oliver Simpson was bent over the desk with his wrists behind his back.

Crisis averted.

"Nobody ever chooses the easy way, do they?" Mattock grumbled.

Sarah was about to reply when the bell sounded above the door. She turned to see three men entering the computer shop. Each wore plain blue jeans and scruffy trainers. One wore a blue baseball cap. His companions had shaved heads.

"We need help," said the man in the baseball cap with a thick accent – Eastern European or Russian. "We need computer help."

Oliver cried out to the newcomers for rescue, but Mattock muttered something in his ear and shut him up.

Sarah raised her Sig and warned the three men to go back outside. "We're with the MCU. This man is in our custody."

"You arrest boy? Why? Why do you bully this child?"

"He's not a child, I promise you that. Now leave, before you get hurt."

Baseball Cap put up his hands like he was in a stick-up, but he appeared unconcerned and made no attempt to leave. "I think this is wrong, what you do. Let boy go."

Mattock barked from over by the desk. "Piss off, mate. This don't involve you."

"You let boy go now, I think." Baseball Cap's eyes bore into Sarah, steely grey and chilling. "That is for best, no?"

Sarah shook her head in disbelief. "Which part of me pointing a gun at you don't you understand? Back the fuck off. Now!"

Baseball Cap turned to his companions. They exchanged something in Russian and laughed about it. Then Baseball Cap turned back to Sarah with a smirk on his face. "Oh, I do not realise you have gun, lady. I think you have, what is word? Nerf shooter." He reached behind his back and pulled out an Uzi. "This is gun."

"Fuck!" Sarah turned and threw herself aside, tumbling across the cheap laminate flooring just in time to avoid a stream of 9mm bullets. She scrambled behind the desk and Mattock joined her, dragging Oliver Simpson along in a headlock. He was bleeding from his arm and cursing so much the Gallagher brothers would have blushed.

"We need technical assistance," Baseball Cap shouted. "Please send out computer boy."

Sarah reached for her phone, but Mattock was already on his. He dialled a number one-handed while pressing Oliver against the floor. A moment later, he was yelling for backup.

Sarah had the only gun, so it was up to her to get them out of this alive. She fired blindly around the side of the desk, listening as the three men scattered. Her enemies were out in the open without cover, but if she leaned out to take aim, the Uzi would obliterate her skull.

Mattock was still yelling for backup.

Ollie shrieked.

Footsteps danced across the shop floor.

Fuck. This is bad.

Sarah and Mattock exchanged glances. For the first time since meeting him, the tough Manc seemed afraid. They were outgunned and pinned down. Mattock leaving his weapon in the car had been a mistake, and she was responsible. She assumed the kid had posed no risk, but it appeared she should have been worried about random gangs of Russians.

Who the hell are they?

"Keep hold of the kid," Sarah said as she searched for a way out of their predicament. She stared into the backroom. "Okay, after three, we rush into the back."

Mattock nodded.

Sarah started the countdown. "One... Two... Three!"

They threw themselves forward, half crawling and half stumbling through the rear exit.

The backroom was a cramped space with nothing to provide cover, but Sarah spotted a fire exit and hurried towards it. "Come on," she urged. "Over here!" She threw herself against the horizontal bar, but the door didn't open.

She shouted in unexpected pain.

Mattock caught her as she rebounded. "You okay?"

"Damn it! It's jammed."

"The bar's broken," said Oliver desperately. He was cowering in the corner, whimpering like a child. "It's been broken for months, but—"

Mattock turned the air blue. "That's against health and safety, you bloody idiot."

Sarah pressed herself up against the wall and peered through the doorway. She exposed herself for a split second and Baseball Cap fired his Uzi. The bullets tore through the wall and chunks of plaster erupted into the air. Responding, Sarah dropped to one knee and fired off a three-round burst that sent the three large men ducking into cover behind the other side of the service desk. There was insufficient space, however, and one man remained visible. Sarah fired a fourth shot.

With a pained yelp, her target fell, rattling the cheap flooring as he landed on his back.

More Uzi rounds peppered the wall.

Sarah ducked back inside the doorway.

Mattock leapt on top of Ollie and flattened him against the ground. His arm was bleeding badly, and a trail of blood covered the backroom floor.

He's bleeding out.

Sarah waited for the Uzi to stop firing, then popped off another shot from her Sig. Baseball Cap's uninjured companion whipped out a handgun and fired a return shot that nearly took her head off. The two gunmen embedded themselves behind the service desk, aim locked in on the rear exit. Sarah couldn't risk another shot.

She had failed to count her rounds. She knew she had enough ammo to put up a fight if her enemy advanced, but she couldn't win a head-on exchange. Her death might be mere seconds away, but it didn't scare her. She had stood on that particular cliff edge so many times before that she had lost her fear of heights.

She looked around.

Mattock slumped on the ground, soaked in his own blood. He was losing consciousness and needed immediate medical assistance, but there was no time to help him. The only way she could save him was by taking care of the two gunmen in the other room.

A grenade, a grenade. My kingdom for a fucking grenade.

The Uzi peppered the wall again, punching loose more chunks of plaster. Gaps in the wall appeared, big enough to see through.

Just think of something smart, Sarah.

She glanced around the cramped room, at the desk fixed along the far wall. As before, she saw nothing except desktop towers, laptops, and various tools. Keyboards and other peripherals littered the desk, but she didn't see how a USB dongle or a wireless mouse could help her.

Wait a minute...

Sarah grabbed the wireless mouse and studied it for a split

second. It was a chunky black thing as big as her hand; heavy, like it had weights in it. It might be just what she needed. She gave Mattock another glance, glad to see him alive but mortified to see the situation rapidly fading. Then she noticed Ollie had pissed himself in the corner. She didn't judge the kid. She'd seen plenty of grown men piss themselves for far less.

"Grenade," she yelled as loudly as she could. "Fire in the hole!"

This is too stupid to work.

A split second of confusion could be the difference between life and death in a firefight, so she whipped her arm around the crumbling door frame and tossed the wireless mouse into the air. As soon as she heard the gunmen swear in Russian, she knew her plan had worked. She leapt into the doorway, needing to break cover to make her shots count before her ruse got discovered. The airborne mouse distracted the two gunmen, who saw nothing except a grenade-sized blur. Baseball Cap rushed for the front door. His companion threw himself down in a protective crouch against the wall.

The wireless mouse shattered on the floor.

No explosion followed.

Sarah swivelled, squinted down her sights, and took aim at the crouching gunman. She pulled the trigger and sent a bullet right through his temple. Brain matter splatted against the product displays. His body crumpled.

"Sergei, no!" Baseball Cap, realising there was no grenade and that his companion was dead, lifted his Uzi and took aim at Sarah.

Sarah rotated her aim and fired again. She caught the son-of-a-bitch in the top of the arm, launching him back against the shop's glass and aluminium door. The Uzi fell from his hand, but he fought to stay standing and glared at her defiantly.

"*Gde tualet?*" said Sarah, using a Russian phrase she'd once heard in Afghanistan. She hoped it meant '*fuck you*'.

Knowing he was beat, Baseball Cap swung the glass door

open and slipped out onto the street before she could aim and fire again. Sarah slipped out from behind the desk and went to chase him, but then she remembered Mattock bleeding out in the backroom. Chase or stay? She couldn't do both.

"Damn it." Sarah holstered her Sig, knowing she would rather see a hundred criminals escape than leave Mattock to die. She glanced around the shop, making sure the scene was locked down. The first Russian she had shot was lying on the ground, clutching his shoulder and moaning. In her estimation, he would live, which meant plenty of opportunities to get answers.

But that would have to come later.

Sarah pulled out her phone and called MCU dispatch. "I need an emergency medical team in two minutes or someone is getting fired."

CHAPTER FIVE

Sarah did her best to stay out of the paramedics' way. Mattock moaned in pain, which was a good sign, but she knew his injuries were severe. Before help arrived, she had stripped off his shirt and Kevlar vest to apply pressure to his wounds. One bullet had struck his wrist, but a second had struck two inches from his heart. The paramedics worked on him in silence.

Oliver kept his distance, sitting in the corner of the room and staring at the bloodstained floor. The kid had had quite a day.

And it's only going to get worse.

Sarah had already updated Thomas and reiterated the need for backup, which was still yet to arrive. It was unlike the strike team to take so long, and she was getting increasingly pissed off about it. Mattock had called them thirty minutes ago.

To keep herself from getting distracted by anger, Sarah went out onto the shop floor to busy herself with the wounded prisoner. Her bullet had struck him an inch below the collarbone, causing pain and misery but nothing that should kill him. That was good, because pain was a useful tool.

The wounded Russian claimed to speak no English, but Sarah suspected he was feigning ignorance. She shoved aside the paramedic working on him and knelt by his side. He stared at her blankly, making it clear he intended to say nothing. The smug look in his eyes was not well hidden.

Sarah punched the wounded man in his collarbone and made him squeal. Then she punched him in the face and bloodied his nose. The paramedic gasped and told her to stop, but when she turned her Sig on him, he hurried away to help his colleagues in the backroom.

Sarah turned her attention back to the wounded Russian. "Who sent you here?"

"N-No English."

She punched him in the collarbone again and made him cry out. "Who sent you here?"

"N-No English. Bitch!"

Sarah chuckled, pretending to enjoy torturing prisoners. "You might think you're not going to talk to me, that you're going to keep your mouth shut and there's nothing I can do about it. But I'm going to tell you why that's naïve. You see, I'm the mad bitch that broke Wazir Hesbani's neck and put a stop to Al-Sharir. I bet you've heard of those two homicidal maniacs, because they were pretty much the worst of the worst. Let me tell you something, though. They both pissed themselves right before I killed them. No man is above pain and fear, so save yourself from the ordeal and cooperate. You won't win this game, because I don't play by the rules. There are no checkmates on my board, because I'd sooner pick up the king and snap his neck than lose to a pawn like you. You want to end up like your buddy Sergei?" She motioned to the dead man lying nearby, his head a mush against the cheap flooring. It had been her bullet that had ended his life, but she knew too little about him to feel remorse.

The Russian muttered, ready to play dumb again, but Sarah punched him in the collarbone and shoved her thumb into the wound for good measure. "I'd say we've got about another five minutes before my team comes and carts you away in an unmarked black van. Then I get to do whatever I want without witnesses. Or, you can answer my questions and go someplace nice with soft pillows and a sexy nurse taking care of your booboos. Your choice, comrade."

"Y-You are crazy bitch. I want lawyer. I want lawyer right now."

Sarah sighed. "Okay, fine, play it your way. What's your lawyer's name?"

"D-Daniel Paulson. Paulson, Page, and Douglas. You call them. I want to speak with lawyer now. Tell them, I want to speak with lawyer."

"Okay, I'll tell them, but by then you'll be rotting in a hole somewhere. *Gulag*, you understand?"

"You lie."

"No, I don't."

"I tell you nothing."

"You just did. I'm assuming this law firm represents all of your buddies, am I right? That's usually the way it works. Maybe I should put some pressure on these lawyers of yours and get some names. Maybe I can find out who your boss is. You have a boss, right? I mean, you don't seem like someone with a whole heap of leadership qualities."

"Fuck you." He managed a pained chuckle. "You have to get lawyer. You cannot torture and tell me these lies. UK are the good guys, no?" He laughed again as if he had said something absurd.

He was right, of course. Sarah was totally bluffing. Once the transport arrived, the prisoner would be taken to an interview room where things would achingly proceed by the book. The only chance she had to extract answers was now, while he was bleeding and in pain. She pulled out her Sig and placed it against his guts. "Does anyone really know how many times I shot you? I mean, the paramedics might make a fuss, but it's easy to scare gentle souls like them into keeping quiet. How about I plug you again and watch you bleed out before help arrives? Then I'll go visit this law firm of yours and see if I can get the answers I need there. Even if you were to somehow miraculously survive, you're going to have a nice stay in one of Her Majesty's prisons, where I assume there'll be certain dangers for you. Your boss might want to ensure you stay silent. For good." She shrugged. "What kind of man do you work for? Is he the understanding sort?"

Sarah was assuming much, but she understood enough about violent criminals to know they were rarely sentimental.

"If I tell anything, I die."

"Tell me what I need to know and I'll make sure you end up on a nice warm beach somewhere. What the hell were you doing here today? You wanted the kid, right?"

He hesitated for a moment. "Yes."

"Why?"

"To recruit."

"For who?"

He looked away and pressed his lips together. Sarah considered hitting him again but decided it would only send him the other way. He was as compliant as he was going to get. "Who do you work for?"

He declined to answer.

Sarah took a shot. Lately, one particular Russian had been popping up on her radar consistently. She spoke his name. "Is it Maxim Ivanov?"

The man flinched.

Sarah put a hand on his trembling leg and gave him a reassuring squeeze. "Just nod."

He nodded.

"Okay, good. Now we're getting somewhere. Now I need to know where to find—"

The bell above the door sounded and a trio of armed police officers entered the shop, their jackboots clunking on the laminate floor. They were equipped with MP5s but left them hanging loose by their straps. The officer in charge, a tall man with large green eyes, put up a hand and told her, "We're here to take this man into protective custody."

Sarah stood and faced the intruders. "I'm with the MCU,

and I've already arranged transportation for this prisoner. It'll be here any moment."

"I suggest you tell it to head back home. Our orders came directly from the Home Office and we've been dispatched here to take this man into custody and keep him secure."

Sarah hissed. "I'm trying to investigate the plane crash this morning. Do you really want to get in my way?"

The officer took a step forward, but rather than confront her aggressively, he moved her away and spoke quietly so his colleagues couldn't hear. "Look, I appreciate what you're saying, but I'm going to carry out my orders, okay? All I can say is that this guy must have friends in high places because the Home Secretary herself has got involved. Plus, his lawyers are already on the case, making trouble. They're insinuating you used unnecessary brutality." He peered sideways at the dead body in the room.

"That's ridiculous. How did they even find out about this so quickly?"

"I don't know. I'm sorry for stepping on your toes, but you'll have to take it up with someone else, okay? Just giving you a heads-up because I respect the MCU and the work it does. It's Sarah, right?"

Sarah grunted. "I have a face that's hard to forget, right?"

"It has more to do with you jumping out of a helicopter above the Thames. I watched that whole thing on the news."

"Long time ago now," she said. "I doubt my body would allow me to get away with a stunt like that now."

"Your body looks fine to me."

An awkward silence settled. Flirtation had become alien to Sarah, and the officer appeared mortified by what he had said.

"I, um..."

"What's your name?" she asked.

"Matt. I'm with SCO19."

Sarah gave an appreciative nod. SCO19 was the

Metropolitan Police's armed response unit. An elite group of officers.

But what are they doing in Ipswich?

"Look, Matt, I appreciate the heads-up, but don't be offended if I kick your door in later and take this guy back. I shot him, so I should get him."

"Not sure that's how it works." He flashed a set of straight white teeth at her as he smiled. "But I'll be ready to hand him over."

Sarah nodded. There was little she could do, so she stood back.

Sometimes it felt like there were too many chefs adding salt to the law enforcement stew, but mostly they were on the same side. She was in no position to take on three heavily armed police officers, so she wasn't going to try.

"Hey," she shouted as they carried her prisoner away, "what about the dead guy?"

"All yours," said Matt, and he exited the shop.

"Gee, thanks. I suppose I'll go and—"

Three paramedics wheeled Mattock out from the backroom on a gurney. The one Sarah had pulled a gun on averted his eyes and flinched when she came close. She had no interest in the paramedics, though. She wanted to check on her friend.

Mattock was half-conscious, with a blood-speckled oxygen mask over his mouth and nose. There was no way he could hold a conversation, so she simply put her hand on his knee. "Next time bring a gun, you muppet."

Mattock lifted his arm and gave her the middle finger.

"I'm sorry," she said.

His arm flopped back to the gurney.

Sarah sighed as the paramedics wheeled him away, but then she got her head back in the game. While she had gained little to no intel from the wounded prisoner, she hadn't come here to investigate Eastern-European thugs. She had come to find a kid with the skills to crash a jumbo jet.

A banging sound alerted Sarah to the backroom just as she'd been about to head there anyway. There had been no danger of Oliver escaping when she'd left him sitting in a pool of his own urine, but she hurried now, suddenly anxious. The cramped backroom was a disaster zone, with chunks of plaster and bloodstained dust all over the floor. One laptop on the desk had a bullet hole right through the centre of its screen. "I think that's beyond repair," she said, and turned to talk to Oliver.

But the kid was gone.

The broken fire exit door hung open, letting in frigid air. It slowly swung shut.

"Damn it!" Sarah threw herself out of the exit and found herself standing in a small yard behind the shop. Oliver couldn't have gone far. He only had a ten-second head start.

She rushed forward into the road and looked left and right. Traffic whizzed by in both directions, and there was a small covered market on the far side of the road. Pedestrians rushed back and forth, carrying shopping bags and hauling backpacks.

Sarah stopped, knowing a chase would do her no good. Even if she knew which direction Oliver Simpson had gone, the teenager was probably faster than she was at a battered and beaten forty. She pulled out her phone and made a call. "Jessica? I've lost both prisoners. One to some kind of political power play and another to my own goddamn stupidity. I need all teams on me, right now. We need to find Oliver Simpson."

"Jesus, Sarah, what happened?"

"There's no time to explain, but I screwed up, okay? Just get everyone out here. And get Thomas on the line with somebody at the Home Office. They have our prisoner."

"Okay, Sarah, but I need to—"

The line went dead.

Sarah tutted, frowned, and quickly redialled. Her phone had lost its signal, doing nothing now except beep at her irritably. She stared at the screen, failing to make sense of it. There wasn't even a signal bar.

What the hell?

Oliver made it through the covered market and hopped on a bus. His heart thudded against his ribs as he took a seat. He was certain the woman with the scarred face would appear at any moment and arrest him.

Sarah, she said her name was Sarah.

When the bus pulled away, he realised he had escaped.

But it's only a matter of time before they catch me.

Still frantic, he pulled his smartphone out of his trouser pocket and plunged himself into the only world he knew – the one place he wielded any kind of power. Using a variety of tools in tandem, he hacked into the local cellular masts and deactivated them. He had learned to do so months ago now, but he had never messed with anything before that could land him in trouble. Things couldn't get any worse now, though, so there was no reason not to do whatever he needed. It was ridiculously easy to access and disable the transmitters.

Just like it was easy hacking into that plane. They should have done a better job of securing it. They're to blame as much as I am.

With the teeniest spark of delight, Oliver looked up to see several passengers on the bus groan and tap at their phones. Hopefully, the disruption would prevent the police from organising an immediate effort to apprehend him. He was safe for now. He could relax.

The smell of his own urine brought him out of his thoughts. At the computer shop he had been so terrified – so sure he was going to die – that he had regressed into a trembling child. His mind switched off completely and all he could feel was fear.

Then, all the shooting and the shouting had stopped, and paramedics were suddenly everywhere. Blood was everywhere. A nightmare, except he was fully awake.

When the paramedics wheeled the scary northerner out of the backroom on a gurney, Oliver had suddenly found himself alone. Mortal terror demanded he flee, to escape the chaos and blood and people who wanted to hurt him. And so he had obeyed, grabbing the claw hammer that hung from a hook beside the fire exit and using it to pry open the broken catch. It had been no lie when he'd explained the fire door was broken, but he hadn't added that he knew a workaround to open it.

He had rushed out into the yard, but then he had paused.

Where the hell do I go? The police know who I am. They know what I did.

And who the hell were those men? They sounded Polish or Russian or something. They were after me. Why?

I want to go home.

I want my mum.

Oliver caught buses all the time, so he quickly realised he was going the wrong way. At the next stop he would get off and head for the bus station. From there he would travel home, praying he didn't get caught first. All he wanted, before his entire existence came crashing down around him, was a hug from his mother. Once he had that, he would accept whatever came next.

There was no avoiding it.

I deserve to be punished for what I did.

The strike team turned up five minutes later, claiming to have come as fast as they were able. Sarah wished she had kept better track of time so she could verify exactly how long they had taken to respond to the distress call, but she was in no doubt that it was *too* long. Worry nagged at her, a fear that the strike team may not have got the call when it had been made. She needed to find out who Mattock had spoken to on the radio.

I'll have to wait until he's in better shape.

As well as creating dead bodies, the strike team also cleaned them up, which was a good thing, because the body on the shop floor was beginning to stink, bowels and bladder releasing. The corpse had no ID, so his name was currently 'Sergei-question mark'.

Sarah stepped out onto the pavement outside the shop and waited for her ride. The earlier drizzle had become a light, refreshing shower, and not the storm she had feared. The press, however, had brought a storm of their own. Sarah ignored their attempts to approach her, and thankfully, with armed police in attendance, they were on their best behaviour. It gave her time to think.

Oliver Simpson had all but admitted he brought down that plane, but the kid hadn't seemed proud or defiant about it. He had only seemed afraid. Had he brought down the plane by accident?

Then there were the Russians. What the hell had they been doing there? Clearly, they had wanted Oliver, but why? Had they forced him to crash the plane?

No. The wounded prisoner said he was there to recruit Oliver on behalf of Maxim Ivanov. The kid didn't recognise them either. They were there to kidnap him.

A black 2020 Range Rover Sport hybrid skidded to a halt on the opposite side of the road. The driver couldn't park outside the shop because of all the police vehicles, but Sarah knew the ride was for her. She trotted across the road and hopped into the passenger side, glad to see a friendly face after being shot at and nearly killed.

"Hey, Mandy. Thanks for getting me."

He gave her a thin smile, hands tight around the leather-wrapped steering wheel. "No problem. How's Mattock?"

"I think he'll pull through. More scars for his collection."

Mandy released a gush of breath. "Good. Good, because I can't..."

Sarah reached over and patted him on the arm. "I understand. It's okay. Just try to keep your mind in the present. I hate seeing you like this."

"Maybe we're getting too old for this, Sarah."

"Ha! You thinking about retiring? Where would you even go without your licence to drive recklessly?"

Mandy leant forward and started the engine. Staring ahead, he muttered, "I don't know."

They drove in silence for a while before he asked her for a destination. The only logical place was the Simpson residence, so Sarah said to head there. The kid was scared, perhaps he would try to go home.

Scared kids want their parents.

All I ever wanted was mine.

Something didn't sit well with Sarah as they headed along the highway, and she had to voice it. "Hey, Mandy? Have you been listening in on the radio today?"

He nodded. "I always do."

"Did you hear Mattock request backup?"

"Yeah."

"Who responded?"

"It was Thomas. He's back at the earthworm coordinating everything. He answered the call."

Sarah nodded and let the information sink in. "What about the Home Office? Did you hear any mention of it? The Home Secretary got involved ten minutes after the whole thing went down. How did she find out so quickly?"

Mandy shrugged. "An ambitious analyst with a buddy in high places? Leaks are always a problem in our line of work."

"I suppose so, but something doesn't feel right about this. Things got real crowded real fast, and I..." She sighed. "Never mind. I'm just thinking out loud."

Mandy frowned. "About what?"

She wanted to share the end of the thought with him, but once it was out there, there was no taking it back. The situation was delicate; she was hesitant to add additional moving parts. "I recognise this road," she said, pointing over the dash. "We're almost at the Simpson address. Take a left here and—"

Sarah's mobile rang in her pocket. The problems with the network must have been fixed, which was a relief.

She answered the call. "Jessica? We're about to revisit the Simpson residence, so can you... Wait, what? You're shitting me? Okay, keep me posted. Oh, and don't use the radio, okay? I understand it's against protocol, but speak to me first about anything you find out. And get a team out to the Simpson residence ASAP. We're not the only ones looking for Oliver Simpson." She ended the call and put her phone away. She banged her head back against the headrest, gritting her teeth and hissing. "Shitting hell."

Mandy glanced sideways at her. "What is it?"

"Someone just hit the transporter and murdered our prisoner."

"Who killed him?"

"Maxim Ivanov. He's willing to do anything to protect himself. That's not what concerns me, though. What bothers me is that, once again, we're three steps behind. Something stinks here, Mandy, and it's time to grab an air freshener."

"Just tell me what you need."

"Okay, listen. Things are going to get dramatic. Do I have you at your best?"

"Of course." He said it with a hint of frustration. "I'm your faithful driver as always."

"Good. We're not heading to the Simpson residence any more so turn around. Do you know the MCU safe house in Hornchurch?"

"There isn't a safe house in Hornchurch."

Sarah chuckled but felt positively grim at the same time. "Mandy, I'm about to blow your mind."

With Mandy's preternatural reading of traffic allowing him to always be in the right lane on the quickest road, they reached London in sixty-minutes. Sarah didn't enter the Hornchurch address into the satnav because it would leave a record, so she barked out directions. The last thing she wanted was for anyone else to find out about the safe house.

Sarah directed Mandy to a side street half a mile away from their destination. She would have had him park even further away, but time was of the essence. Her chief priority was apprehending Oliver Simpson, but she couldn't do that with her every single move being pre-empted. There was a rat at the MCU, something she had known for a while.

But it's not time yet to put down the poison.

Mandy disliked non-vehicular travel, so he was panting and complaining by the time they reached the end of the road. Sarah shushed him and said, "Untwist your knickers, big guy. We're here."

"Where?"

She nodded to a small petrol station off the side of the road. The pumps were empty and abandoned, but above the shuttered building's ground floor was a decent-sized two-bedroom flat. For the last six months, it had been registered as vacant. In reality, a single occupant had been living there for just over two months. It was someone she hadn't seen in a while. Two keys accessed the property, and she had one of them.

Without waiting for Mandy to keep up, Sarah headed across the cracked forecourt and positioned herself in front of the petrol station's shuttered entrance. She used her key on the floor-level padlock and then stepped back. "Well," she said, raising an eyebrow at Mandy, "be a gentleman."

He raised an eyebrow back at her. "That would require you to be a lady."

"Good point. Together, then?"

Mandy nodded.

They grabbed the shutter and lifted it, a little too fast because it crashed noisily into its storage roller beneath the awning. It caused them both to wince. Sarah looked around but saw no witnesses.

The shutter had been covering a large glass window with faded posters and an aluminium-framed door, to which Sarah also had a key. She unlocked it and ushered Mandy inside what had once been a small convenience store. It was empty aside from a couple of dust-covered shelving racks and the remains of an old service desk.

"Tell me what's going on, Sarah. Why have you brought me here?"

"You need to see it for yourself, trust me. Come on."

She slipped behind the service desk and entered a small stockroom beyond. Last time she had been here, rotting cardboard and other refuse had covered the floor, but someone had cleaned up since then.

Made it a home.

There was a metal staircase at the back of the room. Sarah started up it and bid Mandy to follow. At the top, a short landing led to a chipped wooden door. By now they had made enough noise to announce their presence, so Sarah identified herself before proceeding further. She knocked on the door three times and exclaimed, "Bradley. Palu. Breslow."

The password was something only three people in the entire MCU knew. Three names they each had on their conscience. Victims of past failures.

Locks unbolted on the other side of the door.

Mandy stood close to Sarah, his unblinking eyes fixed ahead. Sarah knew she was being cloak-and-dagger, but it was necessary. He needed to see it for himself or he wouldn't believe it.

The door opened and a Ruger GP100 with a walnut grip was aimed at Sarah's face. She didn't flinch.

Mandy was the first to talk, although he began with a kittenish yelp. "Wh-What the hell? Is...? Is that...?"

Standing in the open doorway, Howard beamed. A thick brown beard obscured his heroic square jaw, and his hair was three times longer than Sarah had ever seen it, but he was the same old guy who had beaten her ass seven years ago before recruiting her into the MCU. "I've missed you, too, Mandy," he said, and lowered the Ruger. His mangled left hand – earned by taking a shotgun blast meant for Sarah – went into his jeans pocket. Sarah often noticed him doing it, an insecurity about the fact he only had a thumb, forefinger, and half of a middle finger.

Mandy grabbed the railing at the top of the stairs to keep from falling. "I don't... I don't understand."

Sarah took Mandy by the arm and led him through the door. "Take a seat inside and we'll explain everything."

Without another word, Mandy collapsed onto an old cream three-seater that took up the middle of the flat's cosy lounge. He stared at Howard as if he were a ghost, which, in his mind, was probably a near-accurate way of thinking about it. "Can I get a glass of water, please?"

"Sure thing." Howard disappeared into the flat's small kitchenette and returned with a pint glass. He handed it to Mandy and waited for him to take a sip. "I'm sorry, Mandy. I wish you'd been in on this from the beginning, but I – we – didn't think that..." He folded his arms and appeared to grasp for the right words. "We didn't want to drag anybody else out onto the ice with us." He looked at Sarah. "I assume something changed?"

Sarah nodded. "It's been a hell of a day."

Mandy put the pint glass down on the threadbare green carpet beside his feet. He rubbed at his eyes as if he wanted to check he wasn't dreaming. "What is going on? You faked your own death, Howard? Why?"

"Because there was a hit out on me." He let the statement hang there for a while but continued when no one else spoke. "In the last year, there have been two attempts on my life. The first was a midnight break-in at my house. Two guys, hired muscle from Eastern Europe, broke in, but I defended myself long enough to make it into my garage and lock the door. I pulled the main breaker on the fuse box, which set off the house alarm. They had no option but to leave."

Mandy nodded. "I remember. You reported it as an attempted burglary."

Howard rubbed his thighs through his jeans, and then sat down on the sofa beside Mandy. "I didn't know it was an attempted hit until a few weeks later, when a clunky old Nissan Pathfinder mowed me down at a zebra crossing. In the split second before it hit me, I saw the driver. One of the guys from the break-in." He twisted and pulled up his shirt, showing a thick scar that was only two-thirds done healing. "Three broken ribs, ruptured spleen, and a shattered elbow. It was touch and go from what I hear, but I pulled through."

"Barely," Sarah added.

Mandy shook his head. "No, Howard. You didn't pull through. You died."

Sarah frowned. "Open your eyes, Mandy."

Howard patted Mandy on the back, compassion in his chocolatey brown eyes. "Someone wanted me dead, so I decided the safest thing to do was let them think I was."

The talking was clearly taking great effort – Howard's body still needed time to heal – so Sarah took over for him. "Mattock and I were at the hospital when Howard seized on the table." She tried not to picture it too vividly; tried not to smell the chlorine on the floors or hear the beeping equipment. "He nearly died, but six hours later, he woke up. Mattock and I were there, and that's when we made a plan to fake Howard's death."

"To keep me alive," said Howard.

Mandy stuttered. "B-But how long can you keep this up? And who would want to kill you? I mean, aside from a couple hundred terrorists?"

Howard and Sarah glanced at one another, but only Howard gave an answer. "MCU Director Thomas Gellar."

Mandy leapt up off the sofa. "You're insane. You're accusing the head of the MCU" – he turned to Sarah, "and *your* ex-husband – of trying to arrange an assassination? What's your evidence?"

Sarah looked at Howard and cleared her throat. "May I?"

Howard shrugged. "Be my guest."

Sarah went over to the large window at the end of the living room. The curtains were drawn, and the only light inside the room came from a pair of table lamps on either side of the sofa. She pulled back the curtains and revealed a wooden board covering the glass. As well as keeping anyone from seeing inside, the board also made a makeshift workspace. Howard had pinned various documents and photographs all over it, several featuring Thomas. Some featured Maxim Ivanov. A few pictured them both together.

After faking his death, Howard hired a freelance journalist – an old friend of the family – to document Thomas's movements, which evidently involved clandestine meetings with Russian crime figures and corrupt politicians. The journalist had also unearthed documents linking Thomas to Al-Sharir, revealing the aid he had provided the terrorist when entering the UK several years ago. Sarah's boss, and ex-husband, had been working a split agenda ever since he'd emerged from the dead. Now they were playing him at his own game. Soon it would be Howard's turn to emerge from the dead, and then they would bring Thomas to justice.

"Thomas is in Maxim Ivanov's back pocket," said Howard after asking Mandy to sit back down. "I have wiretaps, money exchanges, and a whole lot more to back up my claims. The only thing lacking is catching him red-handed. That final nail in the coffin would allow me to reveal myself and put him away for good."

"We've been biding our time," said Sarah. "Making sure we have as much as possible."

Mandy leant forward, hands on his knees as if he were going to be sick. "How did you pull this off?"

"With help," said Howard. "Mattock took care of the death certificate, and paid off enough people to make it stick. Meanwhile, Sarah has been taking care of Thomas, tipping me off about his movements and wiretapping his phone every time he switches it for a new one."

"I did that today, in fact," said Sarah. "At lunch. It's getting too easy, to be honest."

Modern-day bugs were a marvel of engineering, little larger than a sim card. She had put one inside the back plate of Thomas's phone at dinner while he had been flagging down the waitress.

Howard chuckled. His new rough-and-tough exterior made him as much a stranger as a trusted friend. It put heat in Sarah's cheeks. "Thomas covered his tracks about as well as you would expect," she said, "but he has a blind spot when it comes to me."

"Sarah's given me enough entry points into Thomas's life to document his every move," said Howard. "He's finished. He'll spend the rest of his life in prison after we take him down."

A twinge of sadness surprised Sarah. She could never forgive Thomas for the things he'd done – least of all trying to kill Howard – but she knew there was a part of him that had always wanted to do the right thing. The young officer she had fallen in love with in the dust fields of Afghanistan had been a good man with heroic dreams of saving lives and improving the world. Somewhere along the line, his pure intentions had been corrupted. It made her angry and sad. Mostly angry.

"This all started with Al-Sharir," said Sarah. "He captured Thomas in Afghanistan, when he was close to death. Friendly fire struck the bus Thomas was riding on, and Al-Sharir got to him first. He nursed him back to health and made him sympathetic towards anti-Western ideals. The problem was, Al-Sharir couldn't just trust Thomas and release him back to his old life, so he sent him to Russia first, where his associate, Maxim Ivanov, took care of him. Maxim was high up in the Bratva crime syndicate, but he was already planning for bigger things. When he eventually split off to form his own criminal empire, he promised Thomas power and influence, but only if he worked for him. By that point, Thomas had nothing left but dreams of freedom, so he agreed to everything. Before Maxim freed Thomas, he put him to work in Russia and the Ukraine, dirtying his hands with extortion, sex trafficking, and murder."

Mandy groaned. "Making Thomas guilty enough that he could never turn on Maxim or try to go straight."

"Exactly. Maxim has enough dirt on Thomas to send him away for a dozen lifetimes. He has no choice but to do Maxim's bidding."

"Jesus." Mandy put his face into his giant hands and shuddered. "Thomas isn't my favourite guy, but I didn't expect this."

Sarah leant up against the wall and put her hands in her pockets. "Thomas's big mistake was trying to help a bunch of local freedom fighters escape on an unmarked bus through the desert. If we hadn't fired on that bus and left him dying in the sand, Al-Sharir would never have found him. None of this would ever have happened." She laughed bitterly. "Fuck. He and I would probably be raising kids in Florida right now, just like we planned. I wish that made a difference."

Howard knew Sarah well enough to take over and give her emotions a rest. "At first, we wanted to help extradite Thomas from the situation he was in, but as we investigated, we realised he's too far gone. He's been helping Maxim bribe politicians, extort local businesses, and sell state secrets. He's not just a criminal any more, he's an enemy of the state. That's why, when I started investigating the Russian crime syndicate growing on our shores, he tried to take me out."

Mandy thought for a moment before nodding knowingly. "And after your death, Sarah picked up the operation, knowing Thomas could never bring himself to kill her."

Sarah nodded. "Thomas's whole life is a lie, but I think his love for me is still real."

"What about your love for him?" Mandy asked. "I see how much this hurts you."

Once again, Sarah laughed bitterly. She pointed to the thick scars on her face. "I left my warm-and-fuzzies in the desert. Now all I want is for Thomas to face justice. There's no other choice. He and Maxim have even got their hooks into someone in the Home Office. *Novaya Sila* is the biggest threat to the United Kingdom there is right now, trust me."

"I do," said Mandy. "I just wish you had both trusted me. I would have helped, even if I'm only a driver."

Sarah turned on him. "Hey, you are *not* just a driver, Mandy. You're our friend, and a vital member of the team. In fact, along with Jessica and Mattock, you're one of only a few people I trust in this world. We didn't tell you to keep you safe. Thomas has a blind spot when it comes to me, and Mattock could survive a nuclear war, but you would have been vulnerable. Mandy, please believe me."

He shook his head and exhaled, his large forearms resting on his knees. "So what's next?"

Sarah pulled her hands out of her pockets and pushed herself away from the wall. "We find Oliver Simpson, and we keep Thomas in the dark until he makes a mistake. The MCU belongs to us, Mandy. We built it with *our* blood and *our* sacrifice. It's time to take it back."

Howard held up his mangled left hand. "We've all given a part of ourselves to the MCU. Are we really going to let anybody ruin what we've built?"

Mandy shook his head. "No damn way. I'm with you. Same as always. One hundred per cent."

"We never doubted it," said Howard.

"Not for a second," Sarah added, a great weight off her chest.

Your days are numbered, Thomas. We're all coming for you.

CHAPTER SIX

Oliver was within half a mile of his home when he realised there was no way he was going to make it. Police cars sped down the roads. Suspicious strangers lingered on every corner. If he stepped foot near his house, he would be arrested. With a level of grief that threatened to liquefy him, it dawned on him that he would likely never again step foot inside the house where he had grown up. The safety of his bedroom would forever be a memory, replaced by the realities of a cell.

Oliver exited the bus at the next stop but left his phone on the seat. It was only a matter of time before the police used it to trace his whereabouts. Not having a screen on his person, or a portal to the Internet, left him anxious. He felt alone, which was absurd, seeing as he spent most of his time on the Internet by himself.

In reality, he had always been alone.

After exiting the bus, Oliver had no idea where to go, so for a while, he just wandered around aimlessly. Then, due to what must have been a subconscious decision, he found himself back on a bus and heading to Watford. He needed to witness what he had done. Maybe then it would finally be real enough to accept.

The only reason he hadn't turned himself in already was

because he was afraid. He was a kid with leukaemia, desperate to hold on to every last second of life. Once he gave in, it was over.

He still remembered his sister letting go. She'd been afraid too.

Things were better when Millie was alive. Back then, his parents hadn't worn false smiles or drunk too much alcohol. The world had been less frightening because Oliver hadn't been alone. He'd had a sister.

Millie's last wish had been to go on a plane to Disney. His mum and dad had booked the holiday without hesitation, but the cancer took Millie two months before it was even time to pack. After the funeral, Oliver's parents disappeared, replaced by two robots who only pretended to care. Their 'love-yous' increased and their hugs doubled, but they were empty gestures, worth nothing.

Why did you have to die, Millie? Things were so much better when you were here.

You left me alone.

And now look what I've done.

The journey to Watford was going to take an hour, so Oliver used the time to sit peacefully and enjoy the thrum of the engine and the warmth of the seat. He watched people come and go at the various stops, trying not to become saddened by what he saw. Teenagers in love. People with bags full of exciting purchases. Old people smiling to themselves in silence. The many stages of life, that Oliver always assumed would apply to him someday, were all on display – but forever unattainable. He was going to spend the rest of his life with nothing but prison bars and shower beatings to look forward to.

Maybe even worse.

I'll never make it in prison. I can't go there.

I won't.

. . .

Sarah flinched and moved away from the document board when her phone rang in her pocket. She pulled it out and glanced at Howard with a finger on her lips to quiet him. "It's Jessica. Nobody talk." She answered the call and put the phone to her ear. "Hey, Jess, what do you have?"

"We just traced a phone call to the Simpson residence. It came from a payphone in Watford."

"In Watford?" Sarah frowned. "Do we know if it was Oliver who made the call?"

"We didn't get audio, only a location, but I had an agent visit Mrs Simpson to enquire about it and she said it was a telemarketer. A little too much of a coincidence, I'd say."

Sarah huffed. "She's protecting her son. Oliver's in Watford, then. Why? Does he want to see his handiwork up close?"

"Killers often return to the scene of the crime. Maybe he's gone there to revel in the destruction he caused."

Sarah considered the theory but ended up shaking her head. "I don't think so. I don't have the answers yet, but I'm certain this kid didn't set out to hurt anybody. Perhaps the whole thing was an accident."

Jessica grunted. "He *accidentally* killed nearly eight hundred people? Don't think that's going to fly in court, sweetheart."

"I'm not saying he's innocent, only that there's more to this than we realise. Can you send me the location the call was made from? Mandy and I will head there now."

"Will do. I already have a team in the area, but you've met Oliver Simpson personally. You know what he looks like. Find this kid before somebody else does, okay? Alive is better than dead."

"Who else knows about the call?"

"Nobody, except the Charlie Team leader and his men. I didn't put anything out over the radio, just like you asked, but I don't exactly understand why. Is there a reason you don't want to involve anybody else on this, because it's kind of an all-guns-blazing situation? The more boots we have on the ground, the better."

Sarah considered telling Jessica everything, but it was still too early. Also, despite trusting the woman, there was no way of telling how she might take the news. Thomas was a fellow countryman, and her colleague in upper management. Dr Jessica Bennett was as loyal as they came, but her allegiance was not solely towards Sarah.

Sarah cleared her throat and tried to sound casual. "I'm probably being paranoid, but I've been getting the feeling that someone is intercepting our communications."

"What?"

"Hey, you know me, always assuming the worst."

"Sarah, if you think we've been bugged, I need to know about it. If there's been some kind of security breach—"

Sarah cut her off. She couldn't hop into this rabbit hole right now. "I have nothing concrete, Jessica, okay? I'm probably just being stupid, but I promise I'll tell you if I get anything real. Right now, we need to focus on finding Oliver Simpson. Maxim Ivanov is after the kid, and that can only be bad news."

"Maxim Ivanov? How on earth is he involved with this?"

"I'm honestly not sure, but finding Oliver Simpson might give us the answer."

"You're right. He's our top priority. Go find him, Sarah. Then tell me what the hell is going on."

"I promise."

"Good. Because I'm trusting you here. If you're involved in something, don't bring me down with you."

Sarah grunted. "The only thing I'm involved in is protecting this country, same as you. But, just so you know, I would never do anything to jeopardise your career."

"Update me in an hour. Stay safe, Sarah."

The call ended. Sarah walked into the kitchen and poured herself a glass of water. Once she'd drunk it, she walked back into the living room and found Mandy and Howard staring at her. For the last hour, they had all been working together on their next move. Seems like it had been decided for them.

Sarah cricked her neck, wondering how much longer she could keep going on zero sleep. "Mandy? You good to hit the road with me? We have a lead on Oliver Simpson."

Mandy looked at Howard and shook his head in disbelief. "Tell you the truth, driving would be a good way to clear my head. This is all really happening, right? You're alive? All this time, you've been okay."

Howard nodded sheepishly. "Yeah, man, I'm alive."

Mandy remained still for a moment, a blank expression on his face, but then he pulled Howard into a hug, almost crushing him in his thick arms. "You keep it that way, you hear me?"

"Yeah. Sorry we didn't bring you in earlier."

"I understand why you didn't, but if it happens again, I'll kill you for real."

"Message received."

"You ready?" Sarah asked. She was growing jittery. Every second they wasted was a second the rabbit might get away.

Mandy reached into his pocket, pulled out a set of car keys, and tossed them to Sarah, who barely caught them. "I'm not doing any more walking today. You can go fetch the car and bring it round."

Sarah chuckled, tossed the keys into the air, and caught them again. "No problem. I'll meet you downstairs. We're going to go see a boy about a plane crash."

Sarah and Mandy reached Watford and found it deserted. Local shops had closed for the day, and it appeared people didn't want to be out on the streets, probably fearing more planes dropping out of the sky and landing on their heads. Sarah wished she could comfort them, but Oliver Simpson was still at large, and as much as she wanted to give the kid the benefit of the doubt, she might be wrong about him. He could be just another sociopath, already planning his next kill.

Sarah checked her phone for messages, having listened to it beep several times during the drive from Hornchurch. Most of the messages were quick updates from her team, but one in particular caused her to take a moment to read. It was from Thomas, sent via the encrypted messaging app that the MCU used.

Sarah. Just got update. Mattock going to pull through, but damage to lung is bad. Looks like retirement will come early. I know you two are close. Wanted you to hear it first. He's still unconscious, but will contact you soon as changes. Tried to call couple times but couldn't get through. Let me know you're okay.

Sarah swallowed a lump in her throat. Thomas must have tried calling her when her phone had lost its signal. She was glad, because she wouldn't have wanted him to hear her become emotional. Mattock lived for the job, and while it was amazing news that he was going to pull through, she knew him well enough to know he would prefer death over forced retirement. He had once told her that if he did his job right, his eventual cause of death would be a bullet to the brain.

I need to go see him.

But I can't right now.

She updated Mandy, telling him Mattock was doing okay, but omitting the further details. Mandy didn't need any more stress right now, not after having just learned that Howard was still alive.

"Thank God he's okay," said Mandy. He tapped the steering

wheel exuberantly and let out a sigh. "You want me to wait in the car, or do you need backup?"

"Stay here and keep on the line, okay?"

Mandy switched off the engine and reclined in the Range Rover's electric driver's seat. "I'll be here, but you be careful. I think..." He brought himself back up in his chair.

She frowned at him. "What is it?"

"I'm not positive, but I think we might have had company on the drive over. A white van. They're not exactly uncommon, but with what happened to Howard..."

Sarah nodded. "Okay, white van. Got it. I'll stay alert."

"So will I."

Sarah stepped out of the Range Rover and headed towards the crash site. It had grown dark by now, nearly eight o'clock, and while the billowing black plume of smoke was no longer visible, the air stank of ash. She wasn't there to focus on the plane crash, however. She was there to find Oliver Simpson. The kid had made the phone call home several hours ago now, but there was still a chance he was in Watford. Jessica had provided the location of the payphone, so that was where Sarah headed.

She found it inside the town's bus station. The metal payphone booth was like a relic from the past, and she couldn't remember the last time she'd seen one. Where once there might have been a bank of them, there were now only two. Takeaway menus and taxi numbers covered the glass surrounds, most of them faded and colourless. Nobody was using either phone, and there was no sign of Oliver Simpson.

Oliver was smart, knowing they might track his mobile phone, but naïve enough not to realise they could also trace incoming calls made to his home. Just like with the plane, he had been savvy enough to hack a secure system but stupid enough not to cover his tracks.

This kid never even considered getting caught.

Maybe he never expected he would ever do anything wrong.

He called home to speak to his mum because he was scared. What would he do after that?

Sarah hurried out the station and rejoined Mandy in the car. She told him to get as close to the crash site as possible, and sat silently, rocking her knee while he drove. He parked up right at the edge of the supermarket car park.

Sarah got out into the darkness of the February evening. The crashed plane now appeared otherworldly, cloaked in shadow and at the same time lit by spotlights and smouldering fires. It was an unnatural juxtaposition of dark shapes and glinting metal. An alien beast rising forth from the earth.

Despite the death toll, things were calmer than they'd been earlier. People's shock and panic had given way to dejection and solemn grief. The press had set up along the cordon, their equipment housed beneath pop-up gazebos. Chit-chat and squawking radios filled the air, yet the whole place felt deathly silent. Most of the survivors and shell-shocked spectators were gone.

Oliver Simpson would need to keep out of sight. If he got too close, he risked being spotted. His name and description had been disseminated to every single member of law enforcement, and the nation's largest manhunt was underway. It would be a dumb move for the kid to be here, but who else could have made that call? Jessica might have been right about Oliver coming to Watford for a thrill, but there was also another reason he could be there. Guilt.

That would be good. It would mean he has a conscience.

Sarah was unsure why, but it was important for her to assume the best of Oliver Simpson. If seventeen-year-old boys were deliberately committing mass murder, the battle was lost. The world was unsalvageable. She needed to believe there was a human element to this monstrous crime.

Not wanting to stand around and do nothing, Sarah spoke with the various police officers and civil servants. She even cornered a plane crash investigator and questioned him for five minutes. As Mattock had warned, the investigator was cagey and unwilling to share anything concrete. The man did, however, infer that the plane crash was no accident. Sarah already knew that, but when the details reached the public, the shit show would truly begin.

The airlines would blame the government and the government would blame the airlines. Meanwhile, the public would blame both of them and ticket sales would fall through the floor. That, as a result, would negatively affect business and tourism. Terrorism, once again, would take centre stage on the news, draining billions from the public coffers as Westminster battled to restore confidence. The damage caused would go much further than the seven-hundred-plus innocent souls lost today.

I need to hear what happened from Oliver Simpson's mouth.
Then I'll decide whether to take him in alive or dead.

After half an hour of wandering around and chatting, Sarah's mouth grew dry. She had drunk nothing since leaving Howard's flat, so she set off towards the refreshments truck that had been brought in to service those working at the crash site. She asked the vendor for a water, and he handed her a half-litre bottle free of charge. "Thanks," she said. "What's the mood? Everyone must be pretty tired."

The vendor, a young man looking rather weary himself, gave her a shrug. His eyes settled on her scars for a moment, but they didn't linger. "It is what it is, ain't it? I've been watching them pull bodies from the wreckage for the last three hours. It's the worst thing I've ever seen, and yet..." He shrugged again, this time looking downwards. He took a moment before looking up again. "I'm still here, helping out, aren't I? Later, I'll go home and tell my girlfriend about it and we'll watch TV until one in the morning. It disturbs me... how okay I am." He grimaced. "No, not okay, that's the wrong word for it. It disturbs me how—"

"Functional you are," said Sarah, helping him find what he was searching for. "I get it. It's surprising how much we can deal with in the moment, but things can change later down the line. Be nice to that girlfriend of yours, you might need her support in the near future." She turned back to see the wreckage. Speaking over her shoulder, she said, "Suffering is like the rain. It doesn't weigh you down all at once. In fact, you can carry on as normal for a while, barely even noticing. But eventually, if you don't find shelter, you suddenly realise you're soaking wet and shivering."

"Sounds like you've seen some things."

She turned back and pressed the tip of her index finger against her face. "Let's just say... these are the least of my scars."

The young man nodded, as if considering her meaning. After a while, he shook himself and smiled glumly. "You hungry? I don't have a lot left, but help yourself to sandwiches. Oh, and I've been saving this for someone who looked like they could use it." He reached under the counter and produced a chocolate chip cookie the size of her hand. "Nothing like a sugar rush to keep you going."

"Thanks, I appreciate it." She took the cookie and turned to examine the row of sandwiches on the stainless steel counter. Nothing looked particularly appealing, but she hadn't eaten in twenty-four hours. "Mind if I grab a *couple*? I'm running on empty."

"Sure thing."

There were picnic tables set up at the far edge of the supermarket car park, so Sarah trudged over and plonked herself down. Her entire body groaned with relief as the pressure of standing removed itself from her spine. Her eyelids began to close as exhaustion spread through her body. Her breathing grew heavy. She was almost snoring while awake.

I'm going to have to call it a day soon.

Wanting to keep working, but knowing she needed to take a moment to look after herself, she unwrapped the cookie and took a massive bite. It was the hard kind, rather than soft, but it was the best thing she'd ever tasted. She chewed it into a mush and let it linger in her mouth before swallowing. Then she finished a sandwich in three bites. Eventually, her restlessness won out, and she pulled out her phone to speak with Jessica. She considered trying her mobile but called directly through to her extension at the earthworm. Someone might be listening in, but she had nothing sensitive to share anyway.

"Jessica? Hey, it's Sarah. It's a bust on Oliver Simpson. Has Charlie Team found anything?"

"They're following up on a few leads, but nothing so far. Just keep your eyes open."

"That's why I'm calling. I don't think I can any more. I need to come in for some downtime."

"Of course. Take as long as you need. We can handle things while you rest."

"Thanks. I'll check in with you back at the earthworm, yeah?"

"Roger that."

Sarah ended the call and got up off the bench. She turned and headed back towards the car, where Mandy would be waiting for her, but something caught her eye as she moved away.

A group of people were gathered at the edge of the floodlit cordon, many lofting candles overhead. Members of the press converged around them, filming and taking snaps. It was a vigil, something Sarah had never seen before. She crossed the road to take a closer look. A woman at the front smiled and beckoned her to join them, but she declined with what she hoped was a polite smile. As a member of the active investigation, it would have been inappropriate to join in, but she enjoyed standing beneath the night sky and watching. A pleasant, waxy odour pushed away the stench of super-heated metal and charred bodies, a welcome relief. Many of the candle bearers wept quietly, while others sang hymns and said prayers. Those without candles held up homemade posters. One or two waved photographs. Sarah could see it all plastered on tomorrow morning's newspapers.

Pressure built behind her right eye. A drumbeat started in her chest. It had been a while since she had felt such powerful emotions, but it was bittersweet. Misery surrounded her – the worst she had ever encountered – yet she forced herself to endure it, to breathe it in. She gained strength from the pained sobs of those around her. She had been so focused on Oliver Simpson's motives that she had forgotten that they didn't even matter.

Several hundred people had died today, leaving countless families behind to grieve. That debt needed paying. These people, holding their candles and photographs, deserved justice.

Oliver Simpson.

I'm coming for you, kid.

Sarah prepared to leave. In the last ten minutes she had moved closer and closer to the candlelit vigil, but she now stepped away slowly, not wanting to disturb anybody with her exit. She hadn't heard from Mandy and assumed he was snoozing in the car. While some of her tiredness had gone away, exhaustion was creeping back into her bones and making her feet heavy. It was time to go. She needed sleep, and as much as she hated it, someone else would have to apprehend Oliver Simpson. She should have been okay with that.

Why do I always need to be the one facing down danger? I have a team. I should trust them.

Sarah stepped towards the road but paused. Ten metres away, an old man was handing out foil-wrapped packages from the boot of an old Vauxhall Astra. A woman next to him, presumably his wife, was handing out bottles of water. Behind them, a second car had parked up, and even more people were handing out parcels. Sarah recognised what was happening; she'd seen it before. Members of the local community had cooked food at home and were now offering it to those working at the crash site. The same thing had happened during the port delay gridlock after Brexit. It made Sarah smile, further restoring her faith in humanity. The hearts and minds of the ordinary British people were still pure in the ways that mattered.

Like packs of hungry wolves, weary civil servants and spaced-out volunteers gathered around the two parked cars. They unwrapped the packages greedily and filled their faces with hot sandwiches and steaming pittas. One man placed a sausage in his mouth like a cigar before chomping it. A young man grabbed a bottle of water and drank thirstily, pushing his floppy blonde hair out of his face as he tilted his head back. There was something familiar about the kid.

Bite my nipples. Is that Oliver Simpson?

Sarah stood a moment longer to confirm it, but she was sure. Oliver Simpson had broken cover to grab a bottle of water. He was right there in front of her.

You really did come here.

I've got you.

Sarah leapt into action, body fizzing with the anticipation of wrapping the kid in a choke hold from behind. But somebody stepped in her way. She cursed and tried to sidestep the obstacle, but the man went the same way as her. It was merely a passer-by hoping to grab a snack from the Good Samaritans, and when he realised he was in her way, he smiled sheepishly and said, "I'm half-asleep. Sorry."

With no time for pleasantries, Sarah shoved the man aside and sprinted at Oliver.

But the kid had spotted her, eyes wide as if he didn't quite believe she was real.

You ain't getting away, kid.

In his panic, Oliver threw the bottle of water at Sarah. His aim was impressive, and it struck her right in the chest. She shook off the sudden jolt of pain and continued her sprint, but the ambush was now a chase as Oliver took off like a rocket. While Sarah was a middle-aged woman operating on zero sleep, he was a young lad with barely an ounce of fat. A svelte figure didn't always equal stamina, though, so Sarah would stay on his tail and hope he got winded before she did.

Let's see how fit flight simulators make you.

"Oliver Simpson, you're under arrest," she yelled, more to let bystanders know she was an officer of the law rather than anything else. She pumped her fists and leant forward into her run. "Damn it. Stop!"

But Oliver Simpson didn't stop. The kid weaved and dodged on rapid feet, avoiding startled spectators and confused onlookers – including a police officer who tried, and failed, to tackle him. Finally, Oliver ducked into an alleyway behind some shops and disappeared. Sarah didn't know Watford at all, but she imagined he didn't either. With any luck, the kid would run himself into a dead end. Sarah raced into the alleyway after him.

Rather than a dead end, however, the alleyway stretched on in a narrow corridor with an opening at both ends. It was an obstacle course of overflowing bins and refuse, and it appeared some ne'er-do-well had fly-tipped a bunch of old appliances and furniture there.

Oliver pulled ahead, jinking between the junk. Sarah could pull out her Sig and try to take him down, but she wanted him alive, and by the time she set her sights, he would be another thirty metres ahead and still moving. It would be a hard shot to pull off, even for her. The second option was to stop and call for backup, but that involved slowing down and allowing Oliver to get even further ahead. The third option was to keep the chase alive. As long as he was in her sights, he wasn't getting away.

Despite a growing lead, Oliver stopped to tip over a wheelie bin. He clearly hoped to impede Sarah's progress, but she hurdled it with ease. "You're going to have to do better than that, kid," she shouted breathlessly. "Just stop this. Stop running and talk to me."

Her number one priority was getting justice for the victims and their families, but she still wanted to hear Oliver Simpson's story. She needed to understand how a seventeen-year-old could drop a jumbo jet out of the sky like a lawn dart. It was a doorway the world couldn't afford to have opened.

Sarah drew on her inner reserves and picked up speed. She couldn't keep the pace up for long, but she needed Oliver to know that she was right on his heels. At the same time, her hopes paid off as the kid's speed faltered. His sprint became a scurry and would soon become a winded jog. Once that happened, she'd have him. The kid might not realise it, but the chase was over. Sarah's biweekly jogs around the MCU compound had paid off.

Oliver neared the end of the alleyway, his speed continuing to taper. He seemed to realise he wasn't going to get away, because he started shouting back at her to leave him alone, and promised to turn himself in of his own accord. But that wasn't good enough. He didn't get to choose when he faced responsibility. Sarah blew air out of her cheeks and a lengthy stitch embedded itself beneath her left rib, but she wouldn't stop until she had her hands on Oliver Simpson. This ended right now.

With only ten metres between them, the kid finally accepted the futility of his escape. He came to a stop and turned to face her. Unlike before, in the computer shop, he wasn't armed with a screwdriver, but despite that, Sarah didn't go in hard and tackle him. She came to a stop five metres away and put her hands up to show there were no guns involved. "It's over, Oliver. You're coming with me."

Oliver backed up, moving towards the end of the alleyway. She didn't think he planned on fleeing. It was just instinct, his body moving him away from the scarred, unrelenting bitch trying to lock him up forever. His words came out in a blubber of breathless emotion. "I-I'm so sorry. I saw... I saw what I did. It was stupid to stick around, I know, but I couldn't leave. I knew you'd catch me, but please just give me a little longer. I'm not ready."

Sarah had a hundred questions ready, but she found it hard to be tough on the kid, despite what he had done. They were standing in a deserted, rubbish-filled alleyway. A minute to catch their breath wouldn't make a difference. "Oliver, just tell me what the hell happened? Why did you do this?" She put her hands on her hips and took a breath. "Fuck, *how* did you do this?"

Oliver shook his head and stared at nothing. When he spoke, it was as much to himself as it was to Sarah. "I... I was just messing around. I only hacked into the plane because it was supposed to be impossible – like a game, you know? A challenge. Nobody ever hacked into a plane's controls before. I thought... I thought that if I could do it, it would be a big deal. Maybe I thought it would change things."

Sarah shook her head. "Change what?"

Oliver flapped his arms as if the answer should have been obvious. "My life. Sports, girls, friends, it's all so hard. But give me a keyboard and monitor and everything changes. Suddenly, I know exactly what I'm doing and everything makes sense. I'm the one who understands everything and can *do* anything. But I never meant to hurt anybody, I swear. I didn't even know what I was doing."

"You understood what you were doing, kid. Maybe you didn't intend to bring down a plane, but there's a reason hacking is illegal. You knew you were breaking the law, and now hundreds of people are dead because of you. You can't run away from that, Oliver. Your only choice now is how you want to be remembered. Do you go down in history as a cold-blooded terrorist, or do you show remorse and try to help people make sense of this? Admit to making one hell of a mistake, and then devote your life to making up for it."

Oliver grunted. "Make up for it? From inside a prison cell?"

"You'd be surprised what you can do with the right mixture of willpower and regret. I had an uncle named Ollie. He did bad things, too, but he turned it around at the end because he needed to unburden his soul. If you give up now, you'll only be remembered for mass murder. But your life can still amount to something beyond that, if you want it to. You're young. There's plenty of time to add some positives to your story. Cooperate, and help make sure nothing like this ever happens again. Please, Ollie, you know I'm right."

Ollie shook his head and squirmed. He might have been fighting the urge to run again, but he stayed put for the time being. "You're just telling me what I want to hear. You're trying to trick me."

"Nope. Whatever happens, I'm taking you in, so do whatever you want. Just listen to me first, okay? What you did today has set light to whatever hopes and dreams you might have had, but your mum and dad will still continue to love you, and even in prison you can make friends. Life takes many forms, believe me. There's always a way to turn vinegar into wine. Right now, you're screwed – no two ways about it – so let's just get that part over with, all right?"

"You should shoot me. After what I did…"

"In any other situation I might have, but I've faced down evil many times in my life, Ollie, and you're not it. You're not irredeemable. I won't let you die in a dirty alleyway, because you deserve a chance to atone, but also because the victim's families deserve to see you held accountable."

Tears slipped from Ollie's eyes. "I can't atone for this."

"Not all of it, no. But isn't atoning for some of it better than atoning for none of it?"

Ollie swallowed so loudly that it seemed to echo in the alleyway. White as a sheet, he looked ready to throw up, but he nodded. "Will you stay with me?"

"Kid, I haven't slept in thirty-six hours, but yeah, I'll stay with you as long as I can. You're going to be okay. Just cooperate, in every way, and nobody will hurt you. It's time to take responsibility, Ollie."

"Okay, I'll come with you."

After all the excitement of the day, Sarah wasn't kitted out to make an arrest. She had no handcuffs or cable ties and lacked any non-lethal control methods such as gas or a baton. The only thing she had to defend herself with was her Sig, but she hoped she wouldn't have to use it. Fortunately, she was confident Ollie wasn't going to do anything now except comply fully. He had finally accepted responsibility.

She reached out a hand and beckoned for the kid to come to her. He took one step, moving around an old wooden dining chair, but then he turned to face the alleyway's exit. A vehicle had skidded loudly to a halt in the adjoining road. A white van, beat-up and scratched.

The one Mandy warned me about.

The van's suspension rocked as the back doors sprang open, and three armed men leapt out. One of them, Sarah recognised. It was Baseball Cap – although he wasn't wearing one now. He had short brown hair styled into a tiny faux hawk.

Damn it.

Sarah threw out an arm and yelled at Ollie. "Get down!"

"Wh-Who are these guys? What do they want with me?"

Sarah whipped out her Sig and took aim. "They want to put you in a prison far worse than the one I'm offering. Now get down!"

Ollie ducked behind a bin just as Baseball Cap and the two other men opened fire. Sarah dived behind an old washing machine for cover, and its thin metal panels immediately rattled as bullets pinged off them. She aimed her Sig over the top of the washing machine and returned fire, but she had no idea if she was hitting anything.

"Lady from shop. You kill Sergei. Now Cosmo kill you."

Cosmo? Stupid fucking name. "Bigger men than you have tried," she shouted.

More bullets struck the side of the washing machine. Sarah flinched with every hit, returning fire again blindly, deafened by the noise. From the corner of her eye, she could see Ollie cowering behind the bin. Then Sarah saw Cosmo reach over and grab the kid by the arm, yanking him out of safety.

"Help! Help me, please!"

"Leave the kid alone!" Sarah aimed and squeezed the trigger. Her shot missed Cosmo by an inch, but before she could take a follow-up shot, a bullet bounced off the top of the washing machine and blood spattered across the appliance's dirty white top. She fell back into cover, frantically checking herself and gasping with relief when she found the shallowest of wounds on her forearm. The bullet had only nicked her.

By now she must have been on her ninth life.

Ollie continued screaming for help, but his voice was fading as Cosmo dragged him away. Sarah tried to break cover, but bullets kept coming, piercing the washing machine's panels and rattling around inside the drum. Her cover was going to remain cover for about another three seconds.

She couldn't allow Ollie to be taken away. If Maxim Ivanov forced the kid to work for him, a lot more people were going to die. She had a duty to protect the nation, but right now all she could see was a rapidly rising death toll.

If this is my time to die, then so be it. Like Mattock said, if I do my job right, the cause of my death will be a bullet to the brain.

Sarah leapt out of cover and started firing wildly. Cosmo was dragging Ollie around to the back of the van. His two colleagues remained in the alleyway, firing at Sarah, but they started backing away to make their getaway. Sarah's sudden onslaught, along with her now unfettered line of sight, caused the two gunmen to press up against the alleyway walls. Sarah ducked and sidestepped, moving erratically to make herself a harder target, all the while aiming and firing, aiming and firing. She didn't hit either target, but her shots went close enough to send both men running for the van. Sarah kept after them, trying to disguise the fact that she needed to slam in another ammo clip.

The two gunmen leapt inside the front of the van, joining an unseen driver, while Cosmo bundled Ollie into the rear. While it was difficult to make out behind the open doors, it looked like he was punching the kid.

Just leave him alone.

Sarah approached the van cautiously, continuing to move erratically. She loaded a fresh clip and prepared to put three bullets into each man, as well as any spares into the driver for good measure. They were not taking Oliver Simpson.

The kid is mine.

She fired at Cosmo but the van's rear door covered him. If she fired again, a round might make it through, but she risked hitting Ollie if the kid tried to make a run for it. She needed to get closer. She needed a better angle while Cosmo had his back turned.

But before she got to take another step, Cosmo sprang out from behind the van door and wielded a heavy-gauge shotgun at her – possibly a Benelli at first glance. He shouldered it and took aim.

"Fuck!" Sarah dropped into a crouch, hoping through some miracle that the shotgun's wide spread missed.

"This is for Sergei, you bitch."

A powerful engine roared, overpowering the meek grumble of the idling van. Sarah had closed her eyes, but she looked now to see a black Range Rover Sport ramming into the van's rear, causing an explosion of rubber, plastic, metal, and glass. The van's rear end crumpled. The entire vehicle hopped sideways and knocked Cosmo to the ground. The shotgun spilled out of his hands.

Sarah leapt up and prepared to grab Cosmo, but one of the gunmen fired at her through the van's shattered passenger window. The shooter bled from a cut on his forehead, but he was angry and alert, not at all shell-shocked by the impact. These were men used to battle.

Car horns replaced all other sound.

Cosmo clambered to his feet and limped over to the van, where his colleagues quickly dragged him inside. Sarah snatched the Benelli off the ground and immediately pulled the trigger. It kicked like a mule, the stock nearly hitting her chin, but a gaping hole opened up in the middle of the van's passenger door and made her smile.

The van pulled away from the wreckage, its bumper entangled with the Range Rover's front spoiler and ripping free. Sarah shouldered the Benelli properly and fired again, aiming for a tyre. The van sped away causing her to miss.

The Range Rover's passenger door sprang open and Mandy leaned across the seats towards her. Billowing white clouds filled the vehicle's interior – deployed air bags – and he coughed amidst a fog of white powder.

Sarah launched herself into the passenger seat. "Move! Get after them."

"Hold on." Mandy fought to get the air bags out of his face, to get a view of the road ahead, but it was an impossible feat. Every alarm inside the car was beeping at once. The dashboard flashed like a carnival ride. He tried to floor the accelerator, but the Range Rover did nothing except roar and grumble. The electronic parking brake had come on and wouldn't release.

Modern cars were too responsible to drive away after a crash.

Once again, technology was the enemy.

Mandy growled and punched the steering wheel. "We're not going anywhere."

Sarah yelled in frustration and punched at the air bags. She couldn't blame Mandy. He had just saved her life.

No time for anger. I need help.

Sarah took out her phone and called for backup. Thomas answered.

"Sarah, where are you? Are you wounded?"

"My default state is 'wounded'. Alert every unit we have in Watford. Target is a beat-up old van, white in colour, with a squashed arse and a banged-up passenger door. I want to hear you put the alert out, right now."

"I'm going to do it, Sarah. I just want to know first that you're—"

"Put out the alert," Sarah barked, "then we'll talk."

"Okay, okay. Hold on."

Sarah pulled aside the airbag and switched on the Range Rover's fitted radio unit, which thankfully still worked despite the crash. She waited for Thomas's voice.

"All units, be advised. High priority suspect fleeing car accident in Watford town centre. Target is a white van, damaged rear and side-door. All available units, please respond."

Sarah sighed and flopped back in her seat. The air bags were deflating, so she could see Mandy's powder-covered face. He appeared irate, and it took a moment to realise it was the sound of Thomas's voice making him so. She waved a hand and made the gesture to 'calm down'. This was the reason she, Howard, and Mattock had brought no one else in on their secret. The more people involved, the more people who could blow things.

Mandy swallowed, took a breath, and relaxed in his seat. For a moment, the two of them just sat there, in the wreckage, probably looking quite mad. Armed police officers advanced from the other end of the alleyway, alerted by the sound of gunfire. They aimed their MP5s at the grounded Range Rover.

Thomas came back across the line. "Okay, Sarah. All units have been updated. Now, tell me you're okay."

"I'm fine. Running on empty, but I've been in worse shape. Oliver Simpson was right in my grasp, Thomas, but our Russian friends appeared again as if by magic to steal him away. It's becoming a running theme with this kid."

"How do you suppose they knew the suspect's location?"

Sarah glanced at Mandy, and they scowled in unison at Thomas's casual display of false ignorance. Sarah had to fight to keep the anger out of her voice. "They've been following me since the computer shop," she said. "That's the only thing that makes any sense. God knows how, but they knew I would lead them straight to Oliver Simpson."

"They were following you all day without you noticing?" Thomas sounded incredulous. "Seems unlikely."

"Maybe they're getting help from someone inside."

Sarah and Mandy exchanged another glance. It was a good thing Thomas couldn't see them.

"You mean law enforcement? You think someone in the police is working with these Russians? Jesus, Sarah."

She rolled her eyes but kept her voice even. "Yeah, something like that. Right now, all I care about is reacquiring Oliver Simpson. The kid still has a conscience, but he's hanging on by a thread. If Maxim Ivanov gets his hooks into him, it won't be long before he takes a one-way road to Hell."

It's not as if Maxim hasn't brainwashed people before.
Like you, Thomas.

"That won't happen, Sarah. Maxim's men have nowhere to go. We'll bring them in."

Sarah sighed. "Maxim Ivanov has hideouts all over the South East. If there are any nearby, Oliver Simpson will disappear, and we'll be left poking at our haemorrhoids."

Mandy nudged Sarah, seeming to want permission to talk. She nodded, so he cleared his throat to speak. "Um, boss? It's Mandy."

"Mandy, is everything okay?"

"Right as rain, but listen, I reckon I might have spotted Ivanov's guys a few minutes before they made their move."

There was a brief pause before Thomas spoke again. "What do you mean?"

"On the motorway, I thought I saw a white van following us. I saw it again in Watford, so I walked on over and hid in the entranceway to one of those nail bar thingies. The van had its windows rolled down, so I overheard the occupants talking."

"You left the car to investigate? That's unlike you, Mandy."

Mandy appeared irritated by the statement, but he kept it out of his voice. "There was no one else around, and I have field certification like everybody else."

"Of course. Okay, Mandy. What did these men in the white van say?"

"They had pretty thick accents, but I heard them say something about..." Mandy suddenly turned to Sarah in a panic. He had clearly only planned so far ahead.

"A garage," said Sarah, knowing Maxim owned several and that it would add plausibility to the made-up narrative.

Mandy nodded and silently thanked her. "That's right," he said. "They mentioned a garage. Said they were going to deliver the cargo there. At the time I assumed they meant car parts, or maybe even drugs, but..."

Thomas cleared his throat. "But they might have been talking about Oliver Simpson?"

"Yeah, I think so. Anyway, when they took off in the van, I got back in the car and went after them. Good thing, too, because Sarah was seconds away from a shotgun blast to the face."

"He saved my life," said Sarah, smiling warmly at her colleague. "Not for the first time."

"Good work, Mandy," Thomas said. "I'll act on this new information right away, but in the meantime, both of you sit tight and wait for help to arrive."

"It already has," said Sarah, staring out the shattered passenger side window at the armed police officer approaching. Astonishingly, it was the man who had taken the Russian prisoner out of her custody earlier.

Matt with SCO19. What are the odds?

When Matt saw her, he frowned. "Agent Stone?"

"Got to go," said Sarah, and she ended the call with Thomas. Smiling awkwardly, she leant an elbow on the windowsill. "I understand you're probably going to want some answers, but do you mind if I make a quick five-minute call? I'm not going anywhere, I promise."

Matt chuckled, looking even more handsome than before. "I suppose you're not. Okay, go ahead, but do I need to call an ambulance first?"

Sarah checked herself over and shook her head. "We're both fine. I really need to make that call."

Matt nodded and stepped back.

Mandy had come up with the plan on the fly, and while they hadn't discussed it, Sarah knew exactly what to do next. She made a call to a certain friend who lived above a petrol station.

"Hey, Bernie," she said once the line opened. "You there?"

"Is that you, Freddie?"

"Yeah, you busy?"

"I wish. What do you need? You've never called me directly before."

"It's an emergency. Is that wiretap I installed on Brody's phone still active?"

"Brody?" He paused for a moment. "Oh, yeah, the Homeland thing. Um, yeah, he's still using the same phone. In fact, he's connecting a call right now."

"We need to listen. Our faithful driver fed Brody some breadcrumbs. Now I want to see where he shits them out."

"Okay, hold on. I'll put you on loudspeaker."

Sarah and Mandy sat back and waited. He looked at her quizzically. "Freddie?"

She pointed to her scars. "Krueger."

"Oh. And Bernie?"

"Think about it."

"Okay," said Howard. "I'm opening the wiretap software now. Can you hear?"

Thomas's voice came over the radio, clear as day.

"Yeah, we've got it. Turn it up."

"—idiots have got every police officer in the area searching for them."

"You put out an alert?" Maxim raged. "You fool. How did you allow this to happen?"

"I had no choice. One of my agents is on the ground and your men shot at her. If I hadn't put out the alert, she would have done it herself."

"*Her?* You speak of Agent Stone. Your woman?"

Sarah grimaced.

"It doesn't matter who it was," said Thomas. "What matters is that one of my agents surveilled your men and has a lead on their destination. There'll be police officers at all of your garages within the hour. Just a heads-up."

Maxim bellowed down the phone, nearly incomprehensible for a moment. "This is unacceptable. If any more of my men are apprehended, I will hold you accountable. Do you know how hard it was to clean up today's mistakes? The Mad Scot is not someone I enjoy having to thank."

Sarah and Mandy looked at each other.

Mad Scot? Never heard of him, but is that who murdered my prisoner?

"I understand, Maxim, but I told you not to get involved in this. The MCU has a lot of moving parts. I can't always do what you're asking. It's unrealistic for you to expect so."

"Then perhaps we should rethink our friendship."

"Fine." Thomas sounded defiant. "You want to kill me or expose me, then do it, because I've had enough. I promise you, though, that I'll take you down with me, you fucking psychopath."

Sarah was surprised by what she was hearing. Mandy appeared conflicted as well. Thomas was their enemy, but he had also been their colleague for the last five-plus years.

Silence filled the line. It sounded as if the call might have ended, but then Maxim spoke again. There was a haughtiness to his tone, replacing some of the fury. "My brother, we have been through much together, no? Perhaps I have shown you too little respect. Inside that sad little shell that came to me from desert is heart of bear. That is good."

"I'm not being your puppet, Maxim."

"I understand. A bear can only be poked so many times before he bites, no? You are meant for better things, Thomas. I shall free you from shackles."

Thomas flooded the line with breath – either from relief or frustration. "Good."

"Yes. I see you are conflicted about role in life. You are bear who thinks is pig, and you are man in love, greatest of all weaknesses. I shall fix for you."

"What? What do you mean, Maxim?"

"I shall render heart free so that you and I can do great things together."

"Maxim, if you touch her, I'll kill you. I'll take you apart, piece by piece."

"Thomas, brother, calm yourself. We have business, so let us focus on that for now. I shall have Cosmo travel to my place in Beaconsfield. You will divert any attempts to intercept him, yes? If he does not reach destination, your failure will convince me you are too much a pig, and I will be forced to remove distractions."

"Maxim..."

"Are we still brothers, Thomas?"

Silence. Then: "Yes."

"*Blago.*"

The call ended.

Howard came back on the radio. "Want to tell me what that was about? Sounds like trouble."

"Mandy set Thomas up," said Sarah. "We told him we had intel about Maxim's men. We guessed he would call Maxim to warn him about it."

Howard chuckled. "And now you actually know for real where they're heading."

"It worked like a charm. Do we have intel on any businesses in Beaconsfield linked to Maxim?"

"Hold on, let me check."

A minute went by. Sarah tapped her foot in the footwell, which had been misshapen by the crash. Matt caught her attention and then tapped his watch. Sarah nodded and mouthed an apology.

"Okay," said Howard. "There's a business on the drug squad's radar as a suspected hub for county line gangs and cannabis production. We haven't linked it to Maxim, but it's all I've got."

"Maxim has been pushing out the competition. If the drugs squad is sniffing around the business, then it's worth visiting. Give me the address."

Howard shared the details and Sarah inputted them into her phone. Outside, Matt was taking a call in his earpiece. A moment later, he started pulling at the Range Rover's passenger door handle.

"Shit," said Sarah, pocketing her phone. "Looks like our time is up."

She released the lock and allowed the officer to open the door. When she tried to get out, her body creaked painfully, and she had to reach out for support. Matt helped her, but he had an impatient look on his face. "There's been a new alert," he said. "There's a shootout in progress at the east end of town. I need to wrap this up."

Sarah rolled her eyes. "White van? High priority target, right?"

Thomas is moving everyone east while Maxim's men escape west. Puppet.

Matt raised a silky black eyebrow at her. "Yeah, that's right. I need to get you squared away so I can deploy my team. SCO19 is the only armed unit in the area."

"I'm surprised you're still on duty after what happened earlier."

"What do you mean?"

"I mean, you took my prisoner and then let him get murdered."

He looked at her as if she were mad. "What are you talking about? Murdered?"

Sarah grunted, sick of playing games with stupid men. "Someone hit the transporter. The prisoner was shot. You really expect me to believe you don't know anything about that? He was in your care."

"No! No, he wasn't. I had orders to hand the prisoner over to a special detachment working directly under the Home Office. Last time I saw the prisoner, he was in handcuffs and very much alive. Nobody told me anything about a shooting."

Sarah considered his argument. Someone in the Home Office was definitely helping Maxim, but there was a question mark over this officer's ignorance. He was only a squad leader. It's possible no one had bothered to update him.

I forget how much bureaucracy there is outside of the MCU.
Most guys just follow orders.

"Matt?"

"Yeah."

"I'm going to take a punt and trust that you're one of the good guys, okay?"

He frowned. "What else would I be?"

"A lot of things, but that doesn't matter right now because I need your help. Do you want to help me take down a corrupt official and a Russian crime boss, all in one fell swoop?"

He was still frowning, and the expression only deepened. "I'm not sure. Do I?"

Sarah smirked. "Yes. Yes, you do. I need a lift and ten minutes of your time."

CHAPTER SEVEN

Oliver shook like a leaf in the back of the van. His kidnapper had punched him in the jaw before slamming the door, and it had knocked him unconscious. When he finally came back around, the van was moving and he was lying in darkness. He'd been punched before – by various school bullies – but he'd never been knocked out, and it left him nauseated and teary-eyed. His jaw throbbed. He still didn't know what his kidnappers wanted with him.

It must be because of what I did. They want revenge.
I killed so many people.

Oliver was clueless about where he was being taken, but it couldn't be anywhere good. Strangely, he found himself wishing for the woman with the scarred face. Sarah had been after him all day, yet he hadn't felt threatened by her. Despite the punishments awaiting him, it had been a relief when he had finally surrendered.

But she let me down. She let those men take me.

He lay back on his elbows and tried to see. The cargo bay was empty aside from a dirty scrap of carpet and a rickety wooden pallet. Bits of rope hung from hooks along the wall, but there was nothing useful. Even if there was something he could use, Oliver was no fighter. He was incapable of fighting off a gang of thugs.

I thought my life was boring. Now I would do anything to get it back.

The drive seemed to last forever, his world comprising only blank metal walls and the thrum of an engine. His hands stank of oil. His trousers stank of stale piss. Now and then, voices mumbled from up front.

He was partially relieved when the van finally came to a stop, glad to be free of the boredom, but he also knew things would only get worse from here on out. His future was nothing but pain and fear.

He scooted up against the cargo bay's rear wall and brought his knees up to his chest. Footsteps sounded. The rear doors swung open. Oliver shielded his eyes, anticipating a flood of light, but only silvery moonlight came in. He tried to speak, but two men leapt inside the van and grabbed him. Ignoring his protests, they tossed him outside and sent him tumbling to the ground. He landed on his knees and elbows, shedding skin against the coarse ground. He immediately leapt to his feet and tried to run, but the man who had knocked him unconscious appeared and kneed him in the stomach. A pain Oliver had never experienced before exploded in his guts and he couldn't breathe. He was going to die. The three large men stood over him. They did nothing to help him.

I'm in Hell.

The pressure in his chest grew and grew. It felt like he was going to burst, but then a stunted yelp escaped his lips and glorious air rushed into his lungs. For several seconds he was a gasping lunatic on the floor, taking in every molecule of oxygen he could get. Eventually, he rolled onto his side and went still, praying the violent men would leave him alone.

But they didn't.

"On your feet, computer boy." His kidnappers dragged him to his feet and marched him towards a large building with dozens of broad windows. It was a factory, standing alone in a massive courtyard and backed by tall trees. Oliver couldn't be sure, but it felt like they were in the middle of nowhere.

They're going to chop me up and hide the pieces.

Or bury me alive.

What if they lock me in a basement and leave me to starve?

A flash fire ignited in his guts, and he tried once again to make a run for it. But before he even made it two steps, the three men tossed him to the ground and kicked him repeatedly. He curled up in a ball, screaming and crying, and trying to block out the agony and obscene laughter. It seemed to last forever.

But then a deep voice bellowed and the assault stopped.

Aching, Oliver looked up to see a figure walking towards him. Only a shadow at first – a thick body on short legs – but the moonlight eventually revealed a snorting bull of a man who the others clearly feared. "This is not how we treat guest," he said, offering Oliver a hand with many thick rings. "I am Maxim, but you can call me Max. You are Oliver Simpson, no?"

Oliver tentatively took the man's hand and got back to his feet. He dusted himself off and winced at his bruises. "Wh- What do you want with me?"

The short, stocky bull glared at him, but then bellowed with laughter. He patted Oliver on the back and spoke something in a foreign language before speaking English. "You are very talented boy and I want to offer job. Work hard for Maxim and Maxim take good care of you. This, I promise."

"The police are after me. All of them."

"Ha, you leave to me. I do not let friends go to prison – especially not young men with magic power to crash planes."

"You know what I did?"

"Yes, Maxim knows. This thing you do, is impossible, no? But you do anyway. You do the impossible. Magnificent, that is what you are."

Oliver realised he was smiling, but he quickly chided himself for it. "I killed people. A lot of people."

"So what? Men die. I do not believe in tragedy. The world is battleground. Do not waste time mourning strangers. Think of self, and glorious future with Maxim. We will be great family."

Oliver eyed the three men who had kidnapped him. They certainly hadn't acted like family, but the prospect of them being on *his* side made him feel a lot safer. "You'll protect me? Keep me safe?"

"Safe, rich, and carefree." Maxim covered his heart. "You have word."

"And ours," said the man who had knocked him unconscious in the van. "I am Uncle Cosmo. Your enemies are my enemies."

Maxim grinned. The flash of a gold tooth chilled Oliver's blood. "You see? Nobody will mess with you. You will become scary man. Man people fear."

Oliver swallowed, wondering what would happen if he said no. Deep down, he already knew the answer. "What do you want me to do?"

"Ah, that is for later, no? Take job and we start great journey together. You want girls, money? Papa Max give to you all. What do you say?"

When Oliver considered his options, it was easy to choose. "I say yes."

Sarah thanked her police escort and staggered across the MCU's compound with Mandy, her body running on fumes. Mandy went to wait in the car pool, but Sarah took the lift down into the Earthworm. She nodded greetings to two dozen people on her way to the head section. Several times, members of her team tried to stop her for an update. She shoved them all away. There was only one person she was interested in speaking to.

On duty, Thomas spent most of his time in the command centre, a cluster of executive offices and meeting rooms. Most of the walls were glass, with long Venetian blinds for privacy. The ones covering Thomas's windows were drawn, but slithers of light between the slats betrayed that he was inside. Sarah didn't knock, wanting to take him by surprise, hoping to catch him in the middle of an inappropriate phone call. But he was merely sitting there, staring at his computer screen. He looked pale, and he was obviously jumpy because he clutched his chest and whistled. "Sarah! You scared the life out of me. Ever heard of knocking?"

Sarah widened her eyes and spoke quickly. "There's no time. We need to assemble a strike team, right now. We have eyes on Maxim Ivanov."

Both of Thomas's eyebrows tilted upwards. "What? What do you mean?"

"I've been working with the police and we've found the bastard. Maxim is hiding out at some factory in Beaconsfield. If we raid it now and find drugs, or anything else illegal, we'll have him bang to rights." She leant forward and put both hands on Thomas's desk. She looked him in the eye, trying to appear frantic. "He'll be in a jail cell by the end of the night."

Thomas checked his watch, but Sarah knew it was nine-thirty. They had both been on duty for way too long, but she was hoping his tiredness would work against him.

Just believe everything I tell you. Don't question it. Be dumb, be stupid.

Be my puppet like you've been Maxim's all this time.

Thomas nodded and tried to seem pleased, but it looked more like he was holding back vomit. "That's, um, great news. Let me make a call and get everything set up. You have an address for me?"

"Of course." Sarah slid a piece of paper across the table with the Beaconsfield address on it, which she assumed Thomas would recognise.

He stared at the address, unblinking, then gathered the paper into his hand. He nodded towards the door, indicating a desire for privacy, so Sarah obediently moved away. She wrapped a hand around the door handle and lingered, hands sticky with adhesive.

"Sarah, is everything all right?"

She froze, and turned back with a confused smile. "Yeah, I'm fine. Why do you ask?"

Thomas squinted at her. The piece of paper was in his hand, and he was rubbing his thumb over it in a circle. "I just asked you to leave and you obeyed without question. Not even a sarky comment. Also, you're asking me to assemble a strike team instead of just going over my head like normal. It's unlike you to consult with anyone, least of all me."

Sarah's foggy mind swirled. She tried to speak without pause, to find clarity amidst the grey tendrils obscuring her thoughts, but it took her a moment to put things in order. "I'm just tired."

"We both are." He rubbed at his eyes. "In fact, I don't think I've ever been this tired in my life."

"No, I mean, I'm tired of fighting with *you*. You hurt me, more than you will ever know. More than I can ever convey."

"Sarah, I—"

"Don't interrupt. You hurt me so badly that I could barely take a breath. But I understand how hard it must have been for you, to do what you thought was right, and to go through what you have gone through. Despite everything that's happened, I know you still love me. Maybe I still love you, too, but that's beside the point. I'm here because I want your help. No more going over your head, okay? Let's work together on this."

Thomas slumped back in his chair, eyes agog. "You have no idea how much that means to me, hearing that. I can accept that we might never be what we were, but I don't think I can take any more of us having this wedge between us. Can we start afresh?"

"Big picture, Thomas. Can we just find Maxim Ivanov and lock the son-of-a-bitch up first? We can talk about *us* later."

Thomas leant over the desk and grabbed his phone. He shook his head like he was snapping himself out of a daydream.

"Right, of course. I'll call the Home Secretary and get everybody working on this, but in the meantime, I want you coordinating with the local police. Make sure they keep eyes on Maxim."

Sarah snapped off a salute. "Already on it."

She grabbed the door handle again, feeling the small square protuberance she had glued to the rear side of it. Confident all was going to plan, she stepped out into the hallway and pulled out her phone, opening the app Howard had sent her. It was linked to the listening device she had just placed on the door handle. She kept a small stash of bugs inside a secret pocket sown into her Sig's leather holster. Howard said it was impossible to predict a perfect time to plant a listening device, so it was best to always have a couple on hand. It had worked perfectly, because Thomas was about to eat the final crumb of cheddar before the trap sprang closed and snapped his neck.

How do I feel about that?

I can't think right now.

The app loaded and Thomas's voice came over her phone with impressive clarity. Maxim was talking too, sounding busy and annoyed. "I don't have time right now, Thomas."

"Just listen to me. I need you to—"

Sarah opened the door carefully and silently stepped back inside Thomas's office. This time, she pulled out her Sig and pointed it at his startled face. He spluttered and pulled an all manner of faces, but she kept him quiet with a finger on her lips. She had already prepared a second piece of paper, so she slid it across the desk now.

DO NOT TIP OFF MAXIM!

If you warn him, I will shoot you in the face. Twice.

I know everything. You're screwed.

Play the game and arrange a meeting with Maxim. NOW!

Love, Sarah xxx

Thomas swallowed a lump in his throat and licked at his lips. It was obvious he didn't know what the hell to do. He just stared at her.

Sarah moved over to the phone and activated the loudspeaker. Maxim's voice came through loud and clear. "Thomas? Thomas, why do you call and waste my time? I have young man in my possession, as discussed, and you are keeping me from him."

Sarah felt her blood turn to ice.

Maxim has Ollie.
It's all going to plan.
I just hope the kid stays in one piece.

Thomas found his voice and started talking. There was no way of knowing if he would play along, so Sarah had no option but to listen and hope. "I, um... I can't speak over the phone, brother. There's a team from the Home Office here. They're questioning everyone. They know someone is working with you on the inside. I need to go into hiding before they find something on me, but first I need to dump everything incriminating."

"Incriminating? What do you mean, Thomas?" Maxim did not sound happy.

"You think I don't keep an insurance policy? I have evidence of every bad thing you've ever done, just in case I ever wanted to take you down. You can have the lot, but you need to help me get out of the country. Deal?"

"I should kill you."

"You have as much dirt on me as I have on you, we both know it. It's just business, right? Regardless, I'm screwed and I need your help."

Maxim barked with laughter. "How this reminds me. Your good friend, Maxim, once again must rescue you from damnation. Why should I help you now, Thomas?"

"Because if you don't, I'll hand this big box of evidence over to the Metropolitan Police. You owe me, Maxim. Without me, you would never have gained so much as a foothold in the UK. I did my job, but now my role is redundant and it's time to pay my severance."

"Being of no use is dangerous proposition, Thomas. Men without worth are better off dead."

"I said I was redundant, not without worth. Once I'm out of the country, I'll be at your mercy and I'll do whatever you want. Right now, I need to get out of here fast, and you need these files. Please, brother, I'm begging you to help me."

Sarah was impressed. It almost sounded like he meant it.

Perhaps he does.

Maxim breathed down the phone. "You know where to find me. Come."

Thomas held onto the phone long after the call had ended. He stared at the table, either unwilling to look at Sarah or trapped in some kind of daze. Eventually, he asked, "How did you find out?"

"You spent five years as a dead man, Thomas. Al-Sharir would never have let you see the light of day unless he had plans for you. When it became clear Maxim Ivanov had friends in high places, there was only one person it could be."

"You could have come to me. Instead, you've been working against me this whole time?"

"Maybe once I might have tried to help you, Thomas, but you came after my family. You crossed a line."

"What are you talking about?"

"Howard."

"Oh." He looked down at his hands. Sarah had expected him to deny it, but she realised now that he was too beaten down to fight back. A toll had obviously been taken, a series of compounding moral debts. It almost seemed like he was relieved to finally get caught.

Thomas put the phone down with a trembling hand. "So, what are you going to do now, Sarah? What happens next?"

"I understand you had your reasons for the things you've done." That seemed to comfort him, but she had more to say. "You're going to spend the rest of your life in prison... for so many crimes I can't even count them all."

"You're going to turn me in?"

"I'm sorry." She shrugged. "Also, not sorry."

"You don't have to do this."

"Yes, I do. How many innocent people are dead because of the help you provided Maxim? How many did you butcher in the Ukraine and Russia at his command?"

"Sarah, I had no choice."

She rolled her eyes. "The defence of all weak men."

"You really do know everything, don't you?"

"I've been investigating you for a very long time."

Thomas turned and threw up into his wastepaper bin.

"Jesus Christ." Sarah winced. "Pull yourself together."

He wiped at his mouth and straightened up in his chair. With a curt nod, he appeared to accept his fate. "I suppose I always knew this day was coming. I died in that desert, Sarah. Without you, without my freedom... I never made it out of there alive."

"Neither of us did. For what it's worth, I loved you once for the man you were. The man who risked everything to do good. Because of that, I'm going to let you look Maxim in the eye when I take him down."

"What?"

"You're going to meet with Maxim, and you're going to wear a wire. With everything we have on him already, a taped confession will give us a nice shiny nail to put in his coffin. Then, when I take him down, you can be the one to slap the cuffs on him."

"I'll die in prison. You understand that, right?"

Sarah nodded, knowing it to be true. Being ex-law enforcement was bad enough, but having Maxim Ivanov as an enemy was even worse. There would be a line of inmates waiting to shank Thomas. "I'll do what I can for you, but that's the way the shit breaks. You'll just have to watch your back."

Thomas waved a hand dismissively. "It's okay. At least my final act as a free man will be a good one. That's... comforting. Helping to bring down Maxim won't make up for all the bad, but perhaps I won't end up quite so deep in Hell."

"You're not going to Hell, Thomas."

His eyes brimmed with tears, shock obviously giving way to realisation. "Really?"

"No. You're going to Beaconsfield. Now stand up and do exactly as I say."

Thomas stood up obediently. He sniffed and wiped at his eyes. "I love you, Sarah. I always have."

"Don't make me shoot you, Tom." She walked out the door and re-holstered her Sig, hoping she wouldn't have to pull it out again.

Thomas caught up with her in the hallway. His mobile phone beeped continuously, but Sarah warned him to ignore it. He was no longer head of the MCU. Right now, he belonged to *her*.

"People are going to wonder where we're going," he said, walking painfully slowly.

"So let them wonder. And hurry up."

"I don't think this is the right move, Sarah. You don't know Maxim like I do. He's smart. Dangerous."

"I've dealt with worse men than him."

"No, you haven't. Maxim Ivanov isn't like Al-Sharir, Hesbani, or even your dad. He doesn't do things because of his beliefs or some larger agenda. He's a genuine sociopath. The only thing he cares about is getting what he wants. He has no friends, no family, and no allegiances. If he realises I've betrayed him, he'll slaughter everyone standing close by."

"Then I'll be sure to stand behind you when the shit hits the fan."

Thomas stopped. "I can't do this, Sarah. We can find a better way. I'll make up for everything if you just let—"

Sarah had heard enough. She pulled out her Sig and buried it in his back. "The only chance you have of anything resembling redemption is shutting your mouth and doing what I tell you. You're screwed no matter what you do, so forget trying to talk your way out of this and help me do the job you've been too weak to do."

He tutted petulantly. "You going to shoot me in the middle of the earthworm? Try explaining your way out of that one."

"You want to play? Maybe you're forgetting what a crazy bitch I turned into after you faked your own death and I lost our baby. I don't give a shit. Oh, and there's one more thing, too."

Thomas rolled his eyes. "And what's that?"

"I built this place. When the MCU brought me in, it was days away from closure. Then I took down Hesbani, Al-Sharir, and my own goddamn father. Now everyone here worships me like a goddess. In fact, I've built up so much goodwill, I could probably shoot you right in the face and no one would dare arrest me for it. And once I dump a shitload of files on everyone's desk, revealing you to be the most corrupt official in the entire country, I'm pretty sure the team will have my back." The startled look in his eyes suggested he believed her, which was wise, considering she wasn't kidding. "This isn't about you or me," she said, "or even Maxim Ivanov. It's about a seventeen-year-old named Ollie Simpson. I've seen too many souls degraded by hate and fear, but I can still save this kid. If you truly love me like you say you do, then help me. I need this."

Thomas swallowed. "Okay. I'm sorry. I'm just facing the end of my life and it's a lot, you know?"

"I wish I could say that it's going to get easier for you" – she prodded him in the back with her Sig – "but it ain't. Now move."

Thomas took a few steps and stopped again. Sarah was about

to lose her temper but then realised Jessica was heading down the hallway towards them. She was on the phone but ended the call when she saw them.

"Are you two still on duty?" she asked. "You both need to get some sleep. Last thing we need is a pair of zombies walking around making executive decisions."

"You're right," said Sarah. "Thomas and I are leaving to go get some rest."

Jessica frowned. "Together?"

Thomas nodded. "Yeah, we, um... We're working out a few issues, and—"

"We're screwing," said Sarah. "We all knew it was on the cards, right?"

"Did we? Most of the time, you act like you despise him."

"Yeah, well, after what happened to Howard, I realised life is too short to hold on to baggage."

Jessica's eyes widened behind her spectacles. "Gee, y'all, I knew you had a history, but I can't say this isn't a surprise. Are you both sure it's a good idea, working so closely together?"

"That's what we're heading off to discuss," said Sarah. "After the screwing is over."

Thomas's cheeks flushed, but he played along. "Run things for me until I'm back, okay?"

"Sure thing. I'll do a handover with the night shift when it arrives."

"Thanks, Jessica. I'll see you in the morning."

"Roger that."

Sarah prodded Thomas's spine with her Sig and got him moving again. She feared Jessica would smell the fart in the room, but she didn't, merely bidding them good night and going back to her business.

"That was close," said Thomas as they headed for the lifts. "I'm surprised you didn't bring her in on your little sting operation. She's been eyeing up my job for years."

"I don't want Jessica involved in any of this. She's already going to have your stink on her, and if you bring her down with you, I'll shank you myself long before you reach the inside of a prison."

"When did you get so cold?"

"Do you really need to ask that question?"

"No, I suppose I don't."

They reached the lifts and Sarah put away her Sig. The longer she carried it out in the open, the riskier it was that someone might spot it. Frogmarching the MCU's director out of the building was suspicious enough.

They headed for the surface, standing in silence while it ascended. When the doors opened, the sky was a black sheet overhead. Sarah shoved Thomas out into the glare of the spotlights. "Let's grab a car," she said. "You can drive, seeing as you probably already know the way."

"A moonlight drive. How romantic."

"Yeah, except the only thing in your mouth at the end of the night will be a gun. Let's go meet your boss. It's time for you to resign."

"This won't go how you want it to, Sarah."

"Nothing ever does, but somehow I seem to manage."

"Don't do this. Just send in a team, okay? You can't always be the hero."

Sarah shook her head and shoved him again to pick up the pace. There were various guards around the compound, but they all knew Sarah and Thomas well enough not to take an interest. "This only works if you go in with a wire," she said, "and if I'm not at your back with a gun, you'll make a run for it."

"I won't."

"Yes, you will, because disappearing is what you do best. Taking down bad guys is what I do best."

"Sarah, listen to—"

"Enough talking. Let's just get this over with."

Thomas finally shut up and did what he was told, but he

didn't look happy about it. She would need to keep a close eye on him.

They selected a car from the pool, a brand-new Range Rover Velar Hybrid, and got going. It took off like a rocket. It was time for Sarah and Maxim Ivanov to meet face to face.

Jessica strolled through the hallway, but as soon as she reached her office, she hurried to her desk. She woke her computer and brought up the CCTV feeds. Something had smelled off with Sarah and Thomas; she needed to understand why.

While Sarah's opinion of Thomas had certainly improved over the last several years, it had done so at a glacial pace – and often against Sarah's will. She had once admitted to Jessica, during a particularly heavy 'girl's night out', that she had once loved Thomas with all her heart, but she had never once inferred she had feelings for him any longer. Despite all the work she had put into controlling her temper, there was still an ember of rage inside Sarah that would never be put out. Enough of a flame to prevent her from ever feeling anything even close to affection towards Thomas.

I know you, Sarah. The last thing you want is to sleep with Thomas. Something else is going on.

You lied to me.

Jessica had fought the urge to question Sarah out in the hallway, mainly because she trusted the woman. If she had needed help, she would've asked for it.

All you were interested in was getting out of here with Thomas. Why?

Where were the two of you going?

Jessica selected the CCTV feed for the hallway and jogged back to the moment Jessica had encountered Sarah. It showed their brief discussion, but little else. She paused the feed and advanced it frame by frame. Sarah and Thomas were pressed against each other, but Thomas appeared uncomfortable, squirming as though his back itched.

Then Jessica saw it.

A single frame showed a dark object pressed between Sarah and Thomas.

She's holding a gun to his back?

She's taken Thomas prisoner. What is happening?

Palms sweating, Jessica searched the other CCTV feeds. She jogged backwards and found the pair inside Thomas's office minutes earlier. There was no audio, but Jessica gasped when she saw Sarah whip out her Sig and point it at Thomas's face.

"Sweet molasses." She reached for her phone, about to order a full lockdown of the earthworm, but realised it was too late. Sarah would already be on the surface by now, taking Thomas God knows where.

But that didn't mean things had gone too far. There was still time to bring Sarah back before she did anything truly stupid. Maybe the situation could be contained.

I don't even know what's she's up to, though.

What if I interfere with something better left alone?

But what if she's snapped? What if Thomas is in danger?

What do I do? Heck, Jessica. You want to be in charge, this is the moment.

Jessica put down the phone. Sarah had been a liability from the very moment she had first stepped onto the MCU's Griffin helicopter, but without her, the MCU would have crumbled into dust a long time ago. Whatever she was up to, Jessica trusted that Sarah was doing it for the right reasons.

"I hope you know what you're doing." She stared at the CCTV footage of Sarah pointing a gun at Thomas's startled face. "I really do."

CHAPTER EIGHT

THOMAS DID INDEED KNOW the way to the Beaconsfield business. In fact, he drove there on autopilot, barely speaking or even looking at Sarah. Sarah, meanwhile, sat with her Sig resting on her knee, ready to shoot him if he did anything she didn't like.

Like breathe.

It was eleven at night by the time they reached a fenced-off compound surrounded by overgrown woodland. Other than a large factory, there were no other businesses around. Because of its size and location, the area must once have belonged to a successful company, but now it was run-down and dilapidated – obvious, even in the dark.

Sarah directed Thomas to park the Range Rover a hundred metres down the road from the compound. The two of them stepped out onto a weed-covered driveway, lined on both sides by mature trees. Sarah searched left and right until she spotted someone hiding behind a towering elm tree. When Thomas saw the man, he yelped.

"Cool it," said Sarah, moving over to Thomas and prodding him with her Sig. "It's just a buddy of mine."

Matt stepped out of the shadows, still kitted out with his MP5 and tactical vest. He gave Sarah a boyish smile. "Thought you weren't going to come. Should I be worried you brought a man with you at gunpoint?"

"Yes," said Thomas, desperately. "I'm the director of the MCU. I've been taken hostage."

Matt's eyes widened, and he looked to Sarah for answers. "Is that true?"

Sarah shrugged. "Sounds worse than it is. He might be the director today, but tomorrow he'll be under arrest on about six dozen counts of corruption and a handful of conspiracy to commit murder charges. Trust me, he's no damsel in distress."

"Okay." Matt nodded, seeming to make peace with it. "So why is he here?"

Thomas went to speak, but Sarah dug her Sig into his spine. "He's here because he and Maxim are bros. He's going in with a wire to get a confession. Then you can move in and arrest Maxim and his guys. Is everything set?"

Matt nodded. "I had to send part of my team to the bogus shootout in Watford – I couldn't be seen to be disobeying orders – but I have four guys out here with me, ready to move in."

"That's not enough," said Thomas. "You're going to get us all killed."

"Four of my guys are worth ten Eastern-European thugs, believe me."

Thomas rolled his eyes. "You'd better hope so."

Sarah prodded him again. "We'll work with what we've got. If you don't want a bloodbath, Thomas, then work with me, okay?"

"I *am* working with you. I have no choice."

She looked him in the eye. "Yes, you do. Once we get inside, there's going to be a moment when you'll have to decide what kind of man you want to be. I just hope you choose to be the man I once loved."

Matt cleared his throat. "This situation is more complicated than I thought, isn't it? Should I call for backup?"

Sarah shook her head. "We can't do anything that'll tip off

Maxim, and we can't risk him leaving. Also, he has so many hooks in so many fish that we don't know who we can trust." She glared at Thomas.

Thomas looked away.

Matt took a step back towards the shadows. "Just send me a signal when you're ready and my guys will be there."

Sarah pulled out her mobile phone and looked at it. "No reception. It won't be pretty, but the signal will have to be me firing a shot."

"Elegant," said Thomas.

"Shut it." She shoved him in the back and got him moving. "Come on."

"Wait," said Matt.

Impatiently, Sarah turned. "What?"

Matt's handsome face turned ugly. He lifted his MP5, turned it backwards, and rammed the butt right against her jaw. The pain was spiritual, filling her skull and shunting away her vision. She tumbled backwards onto the cracked driveway, thorny weeds scratching at her neck. The blow didn't knock her unconscious, but it was close.

"Get her gun," said Matt.

"Do you work for Maxim?" Thomas asked.

"What do you think? Get her gun."

"This is a bad idea."

"You want her to shoot you? Get her goddamn gun."

Sarah groped for her Sig, but she had dropped it. It reappeared a moment later, pointed at her face.

"Thomas," she said, her words slurred, "what are you doing?"

His hands shook as they held the gun. "I told you this was a stupid plan, Sarah. Now you're fucked. You're fucked!"

She looked up at Matt, who had his MP5 pointed at her. "So you're a puppet too, huh?"

Matt shrugged. "There's more money to be made on this side of the law."

"Work with us, Sarah," said Thomas frantically. "You and I can have that life we always dreamed of. Once we make enough money—"

Sarah spat blood at him. "Even if I could bear to be in the same room as you, you'll never be free of Maxim. You belong to him. And I will never belong to you. I'd rather die."

"You're going to get your wish." Matt pulled out his radio and made a call. "Okay, boss. I have her. Gellar too. What do you want me to do with them? Uh huh, no problem." He raised his MP5 and pointed it at Thomas.

Thomas froze.

"Boss wants to talk to you. Get your ex on her feet and take her inside."

Thomas grabbed Sarah, but she brushed him off and got to her feet by herself. Her nose was broken, streaming hot blood, which she allowed to pour. The coppery taste of it in her mouth made her angry, and anger was a useful thing to have. "Neither of you will survive until morning," she warned, and then hawked up a mouthful of bloody saliva and spat it onto the driveway.

Matt struck her shoulder with his MP5, causing more pain and making her even angrier. She held onto it all and stomped towards the factory, eager to meet Maxim Ivanov face to face. At the very least, she would spit in his face before she died.

The factory's interior was unlit, and in the shadows, a dozen bodies moved. Several high windows were propped open, allowing in an uncomfortable breeze. The building stank of metal and oil. A trio of vans were parked by a loading bay near the back, rear doors open. Whatever their contents, she assumed they were illegal.

A short, stocky man stepped out of the shadows to face her. His ample gut was solid, like you could bend an iron pipe over it. He was clean-shaven with thick black hair, and as he glared at Sarah, he shook his head in disgust. "So, you are little woman who causes me so much heartburn? Such a broken, ugly thing. I am disappointed."

"And I expected someone taller."

Maxim stepped forward and backhanded her across the face. The blow rattled her skull, and she slumped sideways, blood pouring from her nose. Thomas caught her and held her up. He protested. "Maxim, you don't need to do this."

"I do as I please, and you betray me, Thomas. Did you really think I would believe your silly stories over phone? Did you think I wouldn't recognise this to be a trap?" He turned to Matt and nodded. "Fortunately, I still have men who are capable and loyal."

"I *am* loyal," said Thomas. "I was brought here at gunpoint. Ask him! Ask your loyal little dog."

Matt shrugged. "He's telling the truth. She had a gun pressed against his spine, and he didn't look happy about it. Also, he's wearing a wire."

Thomas reached into his shirt and yanked the small micro-bug from his chest. He held it up, dropped it, and crushed it beneath his shoe. "I have never betrayed you. Never."

Maxim took a moment, then folded his thick forearms and sneered. "So you are not disloyal, merely incompetent."

"Don't blame him," said Sarah, feeling an odd need to defend Thomas. "You're not as smart as you think you are, Maxim. I've been closing in on you for months. Thanks for the motorcycles, by the way. They were worth a fortune by themselves, but the party treats we found inside the mufflers were a nice surprise. We all had a right good time at your expense."

Maxim growled and struck her again. This time, she spilled out of Thomas's grasp and hit the cement floor. Her entire face burned, the bones in her cheeks and nose creaking on the edge of shattering. Thomas protested again, but he did nothing to help her, not even when Maxim started kicking her in the ribs.

He yelled at her like a demon possessed. "Those were my

drugs. That was my money. Nobody messes with Maxim Ivanov and lives. Do you hear me? Nobody!"

Somewhere around the fifth kick, Sarah's lights went out. When she opened her eyes, someone was standing over her and grinning. They wore a blue baseball cap.

"We meet again," said Cosmo, dragging Sarah to her feet. Two other men stood behind him. "Now I get to repay for Sergei's death. I cannot wait."

"Put her with the boy," Maxim ordered. "We'll move out as soon as I get the all clear from the Mad Scot."

Sarah moaned as she was dragged away on battered legs. "You're going to spend the rest of your life in a cell, Maxim," she called back weakly, "and Thomas Gellar won't be able to do a thing to help you."

"You underestimate me, woman. I have men far more powerful than Thomas Gellar on my payroll. Even the Home Secretary herself is at my mercy."

Cosmo dragged Sarah away from the factory floor and took her into a corridor. He opened a door and tossed her inside an empty office. Before he closed the door, he grinned at her. "I look forward to breaking you."

Then he was gone.

The small office was unlit, but a tiny rectangular window near the ceiling let in a sliver of moonlight. Ollie Simpson sat in the corner, arms wrapped around his knees. His eyes widened when he saw her. "Wh-What are you doing here?"

"Trying to rescue you. It's not been going so well." Ollie didn't laugh, but she didn't expect him to. The levity was for her own benefit, a way of balancing the anger inside her. She couldn't let it out yet. "You doing okay, kid?"

He removed his arm from around his knees and straightened his legs. "That man, the one in charge, he wants me to work for him."

"You know what that would mean, right?"

"It means I would probably have to do bad things."

"There's no *probably* about it. Maxim Ivanov is as ruthless as they come. He won't stop at anything less than becoming the world's biggest crime lord. He's a Netflix special waiting to happen."

"But if I work with him, he'll take care of me and keep me out of prison."

Sarah exhaled and chewed the inside of her bruised left cheek. With a shrug, she said, "Maybe. But that won't mean you're free. Once you work for Maxim Ivanov, there's only one way to quit. And it comes with a one-way ticket to Hell."

Ollie stared at the ground. "The alternative isn't any better. I won't survive in prison. I'm just a kid."

"No, you're not. You're a young man who killed eight hundred people this morning. I mean, you get that, right? I know you're scared, but you've got to take responsibility for this, Ollie. You can join Maxim if you want, but I promise you, I'm getting out of here. And when I do, I'll be coming for you. I'll track you to the ends of the earth if I have to. Because that's my job. Taking down bad guys is what I do."

Ollie continued staring at the ground.

"But right now, Ollie, I don't class you as a bad guy. You're a mixed-up kid who did something monumentally bad. I mean, you've really taken teenage high jinks to a whole new level, but you can keep things from getting any worse. Don't go with Maxim. You'll regret it."

"I don't want to go with him."

"Good."

"But I can't go to prison either. You can say whatever you want, but I would rather be dead than that. I won't go."

If Sarah could have made a joke, she would have, but all she had left was anger. She grabbed Ollie by the throat and forced him against the old carpet in the room. "This isn't about what *you* want, you little shit. Why don't you think about all the people you killed and their families for a second, huh? Everything you've got coming is your own fault, so man up and accept it."

She let Ollie up, resisting the urge to pummel him. He scooted back up against the wall, wiping at his eyes and choking back tears. Sarah didn't care about the kid's emotions right now though. She needed to focus on what came next. Her phone was gone and Thomas still had her Sig, but its holster was still in place beneath her jacket – including the secret pocket. She had on a belt, but didn't see any way to make use of it. She was unarmed and stranded half a mile from the nearest property.

"I'm sorry, kid," she said a few minutes later. "You okay?"

Ollie was staring into space, but he replied, "Not even close."

"Yeah, it was a stupid question. Can I ask you another?"

"Okay."

"What the hell were you thinking?"

He sighed and actually appeared to loosen up slightly. Rather than answer the question, he spoke about something else. "When I was fourteen, my sister died. She was ten. Most of the time, growing up, I just ignored her. She was into girl stuff – stupid stuff – and I was... I guess I was into computers, even back then. The thing is, whenever she was around, it was impossible to be alone, because I had a sister. We were a pair. I didn't appreciate it back then, but when she got ill, everything I thought was safe and normal went away. My parents stopped being parents, and my little sister was suddenly this old and serious thing lying in bed all the time. The pain got worse and worse, yet she only seemed to get braver. Right at the end, she told me that one of the things she was most sad about was that she would never be able to grow up with me, that I would have to do it alone. That terrified me. My sister was just this normal, healthy kid, with loving parents, and she never even made it to eleven. After she passed, I just went away. The Internet is really good for taking you away from your life. You can be anyone you want and do anything you want. I decided to break things. The world was already so broken anyway, I decided to get good at breaking it even more. I... I..."

Sarah nodded. "You're angry. I would be too. Family has a way of slicing right into the meat of our hearts. I'm sorry about your sister. It sucks."

Ollie didn't say anything back. He was panting and shaking his head, clenching his fists. Suddenly, he leapt to his feet.

"Hey," said Sarah. "What are you doing?"

"I can't sit here any more. I can't! We need to break the window and climb out."

"Forget about it. It's too narrow."

"We can call for help."

"Calm down."

He tore at his hair, growing more and more frantic. "No. No, I'm not listening to you any more. Help me break the window or just... just shut up."

Sarah rolled her eyes. She unbuckled her belt and tossed it at the kid's feet. "Have fun."

Ollie picked up the belt and appraised the large stainless steel buckle – Sarah had used to wear women's belts, but she found the flimsier clasps were always snapping out in the field – then he folded the belt in half and let the buckle dangle, weighting it up. He leapt up at the window and swung the belt. The buckle struck the small glass panel and caused a crack. He struck it a second time and the window shattered. Glass shards rained onto the ground. Ollie shielded himself with both arms then immediately jumped to pull himself up into the window frame. But it was seven feet off the ground, and the kid clearly had no upper-body strength.

"Give it up," said Sarah. "You ain't climbing out of here. Even if I give you a boost, you won't get your shoulders through. Just stay calm. Everything will work out."

He turned on her, red in the face. "How can you say that? How can you say that? I... I want my mum. I want to see my dad.

This is the worst day of my life." He yanked at his hair. "Jesus, this is the worst day of my life."

"And soon it'll be over, so things can only get better, huh?"

He knelt and picked up a shard of glass, holding it out like a dagger. "Stop talking."

Sarah rushed to her feet, her body so battered and exhausted that it was like moving through quicksand. "Put that down, Ollie. I'm going to take care of everything, okay? But I need you to stop panicking."

The glass shard was only a few inches long, but sharp enough to do damage. If the kid made a move, Sarah would have to take him down hard. Ollie Simpson might have a broken arm in his near future.

But Ollie didn't attack Sarah. He turned the glass on himself, exposing his left wrist.

"Ollie, don't!"

With an anguished yell, he began stabbing at himself. The glass shard made a sloppy punching sound. Blood came quickly.

Sarah tackled Oliver, pinning his arms to his sides and barking at him to drop the glass. She squeezed him harder and harder until he had no choice but to let go of the weapon. As soon as the shard hit the ground, he sobbed uncontrollably. Sarah held him for a second before twisting around to inspect the damage. He had several bloody pockmarks on his wrist but had failed to open a vein. His right hand was sliced in a dozen places.

"I can't even kill myself properly." He whimpered in pain. "Please, just do it for me."

"I ain't killing you, kid. Believe it or not, life is always worth living. Ollie, do you hear me?"

The door swung open and Thomas entered. "What's going on?" he demanded, although his tone lacked authority. "Oliver? Are you bleeding?"

Ollie moved back over to the wall and slumped to the ground. He pulled his knees up and wrapped his bloody wrist around them. He stared at the floor, sobbing quietly.

"He's fine," said Sarah. "He just lost it for a moment. Unintentional mass murder can do that to a person, I guess. Anyway, what the fuck do *you* want, Thomas Gellar, director of the MCU?" She spat the words out like poison in her mouth, sickened by the absurdity of them. She also wanted to make sure she was getting everything recorded on her bug. With any luck, her phone would still be close enough to save the audio. "Me and the kid were about to start a good old game of I-spy. You ain't invited."

Thomas grunted irritably. Sarah's Sig was tucked into his belt, and she fantasied about grabbing it and blowing off his nuts. "Sarah, do you understand how screwed you are? Maxim has sent me in here to..." He couldn't finish the sentence.

"To prove your loyalty?" she offered helpfully.

He nodded, still seemingly unable to say it. "Let him buy you off, okay? Take a bribe, beg for your life. Do whatever you have to do. Work for Maxim and you can have anything you want. Do you know how many gangs he's taken apart? He's cleaning house. He can feed you intel on every criminal in the south. And that's only the beginning. Join him. Join *us*."

"Join you and I can have everything, huh?"

Thomas begged her with his eyes. "Please. It's the only option."

"And how many innocent people would I have to murder, huh? I'm sorry, Thomas, but you and I are different people. Like I told you earlier, there was always going to be a moment when you had to decide what kind of man you wanted to be. I guess this is it." She put her arms out to her sides, presenting a wider target. "Get it over with."

Thomas took Sarah's Sig from his waistband and reluctantly pointed it at her chest. "I don't want to do this."

"I imagine there's a lot of things you haven't wanted to do, but you did them anyway. What difference will one more little murder make? Come on. Shoot me and finish what you started in

Afghanistan. You broke my heart. Now it's time for you to destroy it."

Thomas took a breath, held it, and said goodbye.

Sarah always imagined dying at the end of a gun barrel, but she hadn't ever pictured Thomas being the one to pull the trigger. He looked her in the eye, breath held, index finger twitching, seconds away from ending her life.

"Just do it," she spat. This had never been part of the plan, but somehow it didn't matter. Thomas knew nothing of Howard and Mattock's involvement in the investigation to take him down, so while Sarah might die here, it wouldn't save Thomas. There was a delicious irony in that. Her murder would be the final burden around his neck while he rotted in prison. "Man up and pull the trigger. Come on, do it!"

Thomas growled, and with a pained yell he lowered the gun. "I can't kill you, Sarah. I can't do it." He raised his voice, seeming to shout to someone outside the room. Sure enough, Matt came inside, shaking his head.

"Maxim won't be happy about this," the crooked SCO19 officer warned, then he threw a thumb towards the door. "Get out. I'll deal with this."

Thomas gave Sarah a look that seemed to say a million different things at once, yet at the same time said nothing at all. He slunk out of the room like a scolded dog, too weak to be the one to kill her, too cowardly to keep someone else from doing it.

Matt closed the door and waited. He had his MP5, but it remained by his side. He took a step towards Sarah and reached for her face. "Shit, are you okay? I didn't mean to hit you that hard, but I had to make it look real."

Sarah shook her head, broken nose throbbing. "What are you talking about, you piece of shit?"

He put a finger to his lips and looked sideways. In a whisper, he said, "I work for the NCA. We've been tracking Maxim's operation since it entered our shores. I'm on your side."

"What? I don't believe you. The MCU would have been kept in the loop about an operation like that."

"We *have* been keeping the MCU in the loop. Turns out your director is bent."

Sarah cursed. "Damn it. Thomas must have kept it to himself. If I'd known the National Crime Agency was after Maxim, I would've shared intel. You're really undercover?"

"Yeah."

"Then why the hell didn't you step inside sooner? Thomas could have executed me."

"There was nothing I could do except hope he wouldn't go through with it. I'm sorry, but taking down Maxim Ivanov is my priority."

"That's cold. I'll remember that when it's your arse on the line."

Matt grew restless, looking back and forth between her and the door. "Look, I've been undercover as a member of SCO19 for a year now. At first, I started taking bribes from small-time crooks, knowing it would eventually get back to Maxim that I could be bought. Then, four months ago, he finally reached out. I've been gathering evidence against him ever since, until you came along and pushed the timeline forward by about eighteen months. I'm winging it here, okay? I'll be thankful if either of us gets out of this alive."

Sarah sighed. If Matt had intervened earlier, it might have got them both killed. She understood why he had risked her death. "What are we going to do now?" she asked.

"Maxim is waiting for transport. As soon as it arrives, he's going to go into hiding. I have guys waiting outside for my signal, but I'm not sure they're going to be able to deal with all of Maxim's guys. How is your end of things?"

"I'm not sure. Fingers crossed."

Matt grimaced. "Maxim sent me in here to kill you if Thomas couldn't do it. How do you want to play that out?"

Sarah rubbed at her eyes and winced at the pressure on her mangled nose. "You reckon you can manage a flesh wound?"

He nodded. "You ready?"

Ollie stood up and caught both their attention. "What's happening? I don't understand."

Matt snapped his fingers. "Quiet, kid. Play along and you'll get out of this alive."

"We're the good guys, remember?" said Sarah, nodding at him. "When it comes to Maxim and us, make sure you choose right." She turned back to Matt. "You're really a double agent?"

"You'll know for sure after I shoot you."

She went to reply, but before she had a chance, Matt pulled his MP5 up and shot her. The bullet struck her somewhere low. The pain was so enormous that her entire body fizzed in agony. She fell to the ground, unable to breathe and barely able to see. Her hands moved of their own volition, exploring her body. They came back bloody. She fought against shock, her ears ringing, her eyes blurry. Matt had lied. She was dying.

Matt knelt beside her and shushed her. "I shot you in the top of your thigh. Relax and breathe. Get a hold of the pain. You need to play dead."

Blood seemed to be everywhere. Sarah scanned her lower body until she located the cause of the bleeding. Matt had indeed shot her at the top of the thigh, just below her groin. It hurt like hell, but it had been an expert shot. The wound should heal, minus any infection. Most importantly of all, it was a bleeder.

Sarah soaked her hands in her own blood and rubbed them over her stomach, trying to disguise the entry wound and make it appear as though she could have been shot anywhere from her abdomen downwards. Ollie hopped back and forth in a panic, but she had to ignore the kid and play dead. She bit down on her lip and pushed the agony to the back of her mind. Once she had a hold of it, she slumped onto her side and closed her eyes. And just in the nick of time, because the door opened and someone rushed inside.

It was Cosmo. "Gellar says he could not do killing. I come to take care of bitch myself, but I hear gunshot. What is going on?"

"It's already done," said Matt. "She's dead. Is Maxim ready to go?"

"Yes, Mad Scot just arrived. We need to bring boy."

"You grab him," said Matt. "I'll keep a gun on him in case he tries to run."

Sarah had her eyes closed, but she heard and felt footsteps right in front of her.

"You sure that bitch is dead?"

"Yeah. Forget about her."

"She kill Sergei. I wanted to see her suffer."

"Suffering is overrated, and dead is dead. Come on, let's grab the kid and go."

"Fine."

Ollie yelped. "I don't want to go."

"Shut up, boy. You do what is told."

"Leave me alone."

There was a struggle.

"You come, or I beat you and then you come."

"No."

"Okay. Is your choice."

There was the sound of a beating, Ollie on the receiving end. Sarah could do nothing but play dead and listen.

"Leave him alone," said Matt. "We need to leave."

"Stop!" Ollie begged. "Please, stop!"

Cosmo laughed. "Not until I see you piss pants."

"Please, no, wait. She's alive. She's alive!"

Cosmo didn't reply for a moment. Then: "What do you say?"

"She's faking," said Ollie. "She's not dead. He didn't kill her. He's lying."

Matt scoffed. "Shut your mouth, kid."

"What is boy talking about?" Cosmo demanded.

"He's playing games. Let's just—"

"*I'm* playing games. Check her. She's not dead. She's faking."

Sarah couldn't believe what she was hearing. She'd been wrong about Ollie. When faced with a choice, the kid would always choose himself.

Same as Thomas.

"I have easy solution," said Cosmo. "I shoot again and see if dead."

"The kid is lying," said Matt. "Let's just get out of—"

"You do not speak," said Cosmo. "If she is alive, then you will not be."

Matt sighed. "Okay, fine, shoot her again if it makes you happy. Waste the bullet."

"It is bullet I will enjoy putting in bitch's face. I shall squeeze trigger slowly and—"

Ollie yelped. "Look out!"

Sarah opened her eyes just in time to see Cosmo flop to the ground beside her, eyes glazed over. Matt stood in the centre of the room with his MP5 held aloft, having obviously struck Cosmo with its heavy composite stock. He quickly offered Sarah a hand and she took it, pulling herself to her feet. She thanked him, despite the sharp pain and her pounding heart making her breathless. "I almost forgive you for earlier."

Matt chuckled, although he was visibly rattled by their current predicament. He picked up Cosmo's handgun and handed it to Sarah. It was an old Beretta with half a clip, but it would have to do. She turned and pointed the gun at Ollie, who was now cowering against the wall. "Poor choice, kid."

"Please!" He threw up his hands. "If he found out you were alive – and that I knew about it – he would have hurt me."

Sarah rolled her eyes. "*I'm* going to hurt you. Come 'ere."

Ollie squealed as she grabbed him, and while it wasn't usually her policy to take a human shield, the kid had earned it.

She held the old Beretta over his shoulder, jealous of Matt's MP5.

Matt grabbed his radio and sent a series of squelches over the airwaves. It was a signal to his team. He looked at Sarah and told her, "We're on. If you're the praying type, now would be a good time."

"I ain't."

"Me either, so I guess we get moving."

The three of them crept out of the office and into the hallway. It was empty, but voices came from the factory floor nearby.

Matt whispered. "Maxim has about three million in coke, weed, and guns loaded up on those vans out there. He'll use it to buy favours, and trade for cash while he beds down for a while. He does it every time things get too hot. It gives him time to pay off corrupt officials and threaten witnesses. Once the heat is off, he'll crawl back out of his hole."

"He's not getting out of here." Sarah clutched the Beretta tightly. "If we let him escape, everything he does afterwards will be on us. Every stolen penny. Every death."

"Are you always this much of a martyr?"

"Yes."

Matt crouched at the door to the factory floor. Sarah warned Ollie to stay quiet, and thankfully he did. Together, they waited until they heard breaking glass followed by a loud bang. Two seconds later, smoke crept underneath the door.

"There's our cue," said Matt and he kicked open the door. He immediately swept right, firing his MP5 at figures in the grey smoke. Sarah swept right, keeping Ollie in front of her. The kid wailed like a World War Two siren.

Gunfire came from everywhere.

Men shouted back and forth in Russian.

Sarah aimed a shot and hit someone. The target twirled and fell.

Matt fired controlled bursts from his MP5, moving further and further away.

The stench of smoke and spent gunpowder polluted the air.

More windows shattered. Gruff voices barked orders back and forth in English. It was SCO19 breaching the building. Sarah coughed and rubbed at her stinging eyes with the back of her gun hand. Ollie had fallen silent, but she felt him trembling. Bullets flew invisibly through the thick smoke, each one an angry wasp ready to kill in an instant.

This was a war zone.

"Damn it." Sarah shoved Ollie away from her and yelled at him over the din. "Get down on the floor and find somewhere to hide. Try to run, and I'll find you and shoot you."

Ollie nodded and scampered away.

Sarah entered an awkward combat stance, staying low and constantly moving, but she did so with a limp. There were targets everywhere in the smoke, but it was hard to discern friend from foe. Likewise, there was only one man she was interested in finding and killing.

Maxim stood at the rear of the factory, next to the three parked vans. A pair of large shutters had opened, allowing the smoke to clear. Several men surrounded Maxim, seeking targets, but they didn't see Sarah. She took aim, hoping the old Beretta was accurate enough to hit a target at twenty metres.

This might be my only chance.

She sensed movement to her right and turned just in time to avoid a punch to the side of her head. Evading the attack caused her to lose balance, and her foe snatched at her Berretta, attempting to yank it away from her. She turned, putting her hip between them and trying to leverage the weapon back into her control. Her attacker was strong, but he wheezed like an invalid. She couldn't break his grip, so she turned back and brought up a knee, striking him in the ribs and forcing a fetid gasp from his lips. She went to knee him a second time, but he caught her leg and headbutted her in her broken nose. Her hands slipped off the Beretta, and she staggered backwards, blinded by tears. Fiery shards erupted from the bones in her face. She tried to defend herself, but her senses fled.

Rather than shoot her with the Beretta, Sarah's attacker punched her in the stomach and doubled her over. The weakness in her wounded thigh caused her to topple right over onto the floor, where she lay, beaten. Utterly beaten.

I can't go on. I give in.

Sarah's attacker stood over her, a foul-faced man covered in scars as ugly as hers. "I shoulda slit yer throat a long time ago, wee lass. I'd 'ave been doin' ye a favour."

Sarah couldn't believe who she was looking at. She blinked away the tears and tried to keep her vision from spinning. "Hamish?"

"Aye. We meet again, Captain. Now get yer feckin arse oop off the ground so I can kill ye."

Sarah tried to resist, but Hamish dragged her along the floor by her ponytail. She had thought the man dead, sinking into the Thames after she had shot him, but they had never actually found his body. Truthfully, nobody had looked particularly hard, assuming his corpse would eventually 'wash up' somewhere. Looked like it finally had.

"Why won't you die, Hamish?"

"Vengeance is quite a drug, wee lass. The thought of watching ye die has kept me goin' though many a bad time."

"Just get it over with."

"All in good time." He dragged her over to the vans, gunfire still raging throughout the factory, and deposited her at Maxim's feet.

The angry bull snorted, but then he grinned, morphing into a hyena. "The problems you have caused me, woman. I admit, I am less disappointed in you. Still, you fail."

Sarah looked up and saw what he meant. A line of vehicles had pulled up outside the factory in front of the open shutters. Headlights lit up the night, and a dozen armed thugs hopped out of the assembled cars. Matt and four SCO19 officers wasn't going to be enough.

"Get her on her knees," Maxim ordered, and Hamish obeyed. Sarah teetered back and forth, barely able to hold herself up, flitting in and out of consciousness. She glared at Maxim, wishing she could kill him with a look. He unfastened his zip and looked down at her. "You want to try work something out, sweetheart?"

"You put it in my mouth, you lose it."

Maxim redid his zip and chuckled. "You are ugly bitch, anyway. At least I will not make your face any worse." He pulled out a well-oiled Colt Python and pressed it against her forehead. It was cold against her sweaty skin. *"Do svidaniya*, bitch!"

"Maxim!"

Thomas darted out of the smoke with Sarah's Sig held in both hands. He fired, and Maxim lurched back against one of the vans, his blood spattering the side panel. The men around him burst into action, crouching and firing. Thomas ducked and took out two targets right away, but then the Sig ran dry and the fight turned sour. The first shot struck his elbow, causing him to drop the Sig and his arm to dangle by his side. The second shot entered his stomach and caused him to double over and spit blood. The third shot struck his shoulder and spun him. He collapsed to the ground, body flip-flopping in shock and agony. It had been a valiant effort, so unexpected that it had nearly worked, but this wasn't an action movie.

Sarah held her breath.

Why would he be so reckless?

Was it the sight of me on my knees about to die?

"Stop firing!" Maxim bellowed, and at once his men disengaged, pointing their guns towards the rafters. Maxim gritted his teeth, biting back the pain of having been shot through the left biceps. He held his Colt Python in his right hand, cocking it and pointing it at Thomas, who now writhed in a pool of his own blood but seemed unconcerned by his own mortality. He peered over at Sarah and mouthed the words, "I-I'm sorry. F-F-For all of it."

Sarah nodded, wanting to say she forgave him, but too wounded to speak. All she could do was nod and offer him a blood-soaked smile. It was no way to say goodbye.

Maxim walked closer, still pointing his Colt Python.

Thomas turned his gaze and bared his bloody teeth. "You're finished, Maxim. You're a small-time criminal with a big-time ego. Three years from now, nobody will even remem—"

Maxim fired at point-blank range and reduced Thomas's left kneecap to mush. Thomas bellowed in agony, eyes rolling back in his head. Maxim aimed and fired a second bullet into his right knee. He laughed while he did it.

Thomas passed out. A mercy.

Sarah tried to keep from passing out herself. Even in the smoky gloom, she could see Thomas's blood sprayed across the floor, saw the insides of his ruined kneecaps. She hated him, but deep in her heart, she loved him, too. Despite what he had done, she believed Thomas to be truly sorry.

It was too late now though.

Maxim chuckled. "I think stomach wound will take care of rest. No reason to end glorious suffering prematurely." He walked away, back over to Sarah.

Sarah spat a wad of congealing blood from her nose onto the floor. The gunfire was finally fading, replaced by the wounded screams of SCO19 officers. Sarah's plan had failed. She had set up the pieces, but the odds had been too heavily stacked against her.

I thought I could rely on other people to help me.
I thought I could trust them.

Cosmo appeared out of the smoke, controlling Ollie with a hammerlock. "I find boy pissing in corner. Policeman betray us. Hits me in head after faking this one's death." He pointed at Sarah. "Untrustworthy pig."

"You can't trust anyone these days," Sarah mumbled, hoping

Matt somehow got out of this alive. They truly had been on the same side.

Maxim sighed. "That's the problem with bribing men, they are disloyal in first place. I want that turncoat dealt with before we leave. Oliver, you will come with me now. Do you understand?"

Ollie nodded, pale-faced and snotty-nosed. The kid deserved everything he got, but the problem was that he had the skills to do a lot of damage. Maxim wasn't just escaping with a wanted criminal; he was escaping with a weapon of mass destruction.

"Can I take care of the wee lass now?" Hamish asked Maxim. "We 'ad a deal."

Maxim nodded. "You've earned the right."

"Aye, ain't I just."

Cosmo grunted. He was holding the back of his head where Matt had struck him, and he no longer had his baseball cap. "*I want to kill bitch. It is personal.*"

Hamish glared at Cosmo, his face a tapestry of scarred flesh. "Personal? You dinnae wanna talk to me aboot personal, pal. This one left me fer dead. Twice. I did yer dirty work earlier, taking care of your captured man. This was my price."

Maxim nodded towards the vans. "Take care of boy, Cosmo. Do not make me ask twice."

Cosmo looked at Hamish and said, "*Shluha vokzal'naja.*" He then grabbed Ollie and stormed off towards the front of the vans.

"There's a good boy," said Hamish, and he turned to Sarah with the old Beretta in his hand. "Sorry for yer loss, Captain." He nodded at Thomas's body. "I still remember the two of ye, back on base. Lovesick kids, ye were. Maybe if ye'd focused more on yer men and less about gettin' yer fanny filled, we might nae be here. It's time those young lads ye got killed had their justice, do ye nae reckon?"

Sarah glared at him, wishing he really had died when she'd let Hesbani cut his throat years before. "Hesbani and Al-Sharir killed those men," she said. "Justice has already been served."

"Aye, or at least yer version of it. But what about *my* justice?"

"You don't deserve any."

Maxim grumbled. "Get over with. We leave now."

"Hold ye 'orses. Just let me enjoy the moment, will ye?"

Sarah glanced over at Thomas's lifeless body, thinking back to another life, one full of hope instead of despair. The MCU had saved her, but it had also damned her to a life surrounded by ghosts and demons. It was time to be free of it all. She closed her eyes.

More gunfire broke out. It came not from inside the factory, but from without. Sarah opened her eyes again and looked through the open shutters, towards the collection of cars Maxim's backup had arrived in. Several of the men there collapsed to the ground, wounded or dead. Another sprawled over the bonnet of a light-coloured saloon and started to scream. The remaining men scattered for cover. Suddenly chaos reigned.

Sarah sighed with relief.

Better late than never.

Hamish was distracted by the gunshots coming from outside. He still had the old Beretta pointed at Sarah's face, but he was looking back over his shoulder. Sarah had nothing left in the tank – she already felt dead – but she grabbed hold of that familiar old anger inside her and used it to launch herself upwards. She grabbed the Beretta and rotated her body out of its way. At the same time, she bent Hamish's wrist and forced his hand open. He cried out in surprise and tried to grab her by the hair, but Sarah leapt away with the Beretta now in her possession.

Hamish grinned, mouth crooked, teeth on display. "Well, wee lass, it looks like—"

Sarah raised her aim and pulled the trigger. The old Beretta bucked like a mule, but the bullet did its job, putting a small hole beneath Hamish's left eye – and a great big one in the back of his head. He slumped to the ground, brains leaking onto the concrete.

Sarah stepped over him and shot him one more time in the

face. "You should have learned your lesson the first time I killed you."

There was a moan, audible even over the gunfire.

Sarah turned. "Shit, Thomas!"

Her ex-husband was still alive, twitching on the ground and reaching a hand out to her. Sarah raced over to him, sliding to her knees and hoping the gunfight wouldn't find her. Blood bubbled between Thomas's lips. His watery eyes searched blindly, almost like he couldn't see, but then his gaze settled on her. "Sarah, I..."

Sarah shushed him, placing a hand gently on his shoulder. "Stay quiet. I'm going to get you help. You're going to be okay."

"N-No."

"Yes."

"Just... listen... I-I have what you need. Everything. M-Maxim."

"You have evidence?"

He coughed and blood sprayed everywhere. "I want... I want you to have it."

Sarah nodded, then listened as Thomas endeavoured to tell her about a safe-deposit box kept at an ordinary high street bank in Hammersmith.

"It's enough to lock him away for... for a thousand years." Thomas suddenly sounder stronger, and Sarah grew hopeful. She glanced over her shoulder and saw that Maxim and his men were engaging with their attackers outside. It was only a matter of time before someone came to take care of her. She still had the Beretta, but she was a sitting duck.

"Thomas, I'm going to be right back, okay? The cavalry has arrived and I need to go help."

"N-No. Run. Get the evidence and deal with Maxim later."

She opened her shirt and revealed the pocket beneath her holster. "It's okay. I've been carrying a bug on me this entire time. I recorded everything. I think. Just need to find my phone."

"A bug?"

"Yep. I don't go anywhere without one." She chuckled and

stroked Thomas's hair. Suddenly, the sins of his past didn't seem to matter so much. Maybe there had been another way than this.

"So that's how you..." Thomas's eyes darted to the side. "Wait!"

Sarah turned and found herself at the end of a gun barrel again. She groaned. "I really need to grow eyes in the back of my head."

Cosmo glared at her from beneath a pair of bushy V-shaped eyebrows. His faux hawk was sweaty and flat. "Is my lucky day, no? Now I get to kill bitch who kill my friend."

"Yeah, sorry about that. What was his name again? Sanjay? Sidney?"

"Sergei. His name was Sergei. We were like brothers."

"Lovers? Nice. Well, I'm sure you and Sandy will be together again soon."

Sarah sensed the end of Cosmo's tether and leapt aside right as he pulled the trigger. At the same time, she planted a boot on his kneecap. He howled in pain, staggering backwards, but he stayed on his feet. He pointed his gun at her again and snarled. "Bitch."

"You should really look behind you."

It wasn't a bluff, and something in Sarah's expression must have told Cosmo that, because he heeded her warning and turned around.

He tried to react.

But Howard was too fast. A bearded assassin, dressed in jeans and T-shirt, he unloaded three rounds into Cosmo's chest, steadying with his mangled hand like it was no impediment at all. Cosmo hit the ground and left no question that he was dead.

Howard hurried to Sarah's side, but she shook her head and shoved him away. "You bastard! Why did you come so late?"

Howard noticed Thomas lying in a pool of blood and visibly deflated. His arms flopped to his sides. "I'm sorry. Mandy had to go through Jessica to authorise the assault. It took some convincing, because she saw you marching Thomas out of the earthworm at gunpoint. I got here as fast as I could."

Sarah sighed, unable to stay angry. "We should have brought her in from the start."

"H-Howard?" Thomas was staring at him, blinking slowly. "Is that you?"

Howard turned to Thomas, appearing unsure how to react. "I'm afraid I'm harder to kill than you planned on."

Thomas said nothing, but he released a breath that almost sounded like relief. "Look after her."

"I can look after mys..." Sarah's words trailed off as she realised Thomas was dead. A few seconds passed before she could breathe.

"I'm sorry," said Howard.

"Be sorry later."

The gunfight outside continued to rage, and as the smoke in the factory began clearing, dozens of bodies revealed themselves. One body was moving, a survivor getting to their feet. It was Matt. He stumbled over to join Sarah and Howard, clutching his side where he was bleeding from a gunshot wound where a bullet had made it through underneath the straps. "Took your sweet time," he said, glaring at Howard. "I lost men. Good officers."

"I'm sorry."

Sarah nodded. "Me too."

Matt sighed. "I'm sorry to say it, Sarah, but I wish I'd never met you."

"I get that a lot. For what it's worth, I lost people too." She got to her feet unsteadily. "And I'm not so sure I'll even make it myself."

"Let's just finish this." He shouldered his MP5. "Maxim needs to pay."

Howard turned and pointed to the open shutters where car headlights still illuminated the darkness outside. "He was trying to escape, moving with the last of his men into the woods. I already have a team moving in to flank him. He's not going anywhere."

Sarah sneered. "Let's go put a sword in this bull."

The three of them headed out into the night. Gun smoke swirled in the air, thick enough to irritate her throat. Half a dozen of Maxim's guys lay dead on the ground, executed by high-velocity rifle fire. An MCU strike force had secured the area and was dispelling the remaining darkness with flares and flashlights. Further on, a second team was advancing into the woods. Sarah hurried after the second team as quickly as her wounded groin would allow her. Even running on empty, she was still controlled by her impulses, still determined to be the one who faced evil head-on. Howard went with her, but Matt stayed behind, his injuries catching up with him.

Sarah and Howard caught up with the advance team. Howard asked for an update and shared it with Sarah a minute later, a pleased expression on his face. "Maxim is injured, and he only has a few men left. It's over."

"Don't speak too soon."

Shouts split the silence, voices yelling in English. Something had alarmed the strike team up ahead. "Drop the gun. Let the boy go. You're under arrest."

Sarah broke away from Howard and stumbled through the trees. She found Maxim and two of his men cornered at the edge of a steep incline. To continue his escape, Maxim would have to turn his back and lower his weapon to clamber up it, and if he did that, the strike team would shoot him. Wisely, he had chosen a different tactic.

Maxim had a thick forearm wrapped around Ollie Simpson's throat. The barrel of his Colt Python dug into the boy's temple. "Back off, or I'll blow out boy's brains."

Ollie sobbed. "Please. I just want this to stop."

"Quiet boy. You are ticket out of here."

Sarah limped out from behind a wide-bodied oak. "Really,

Maxim? You think a wanted mass murderer makes a good hostage? I should just kill you both."

"Ha! No, you are good guys. You want to lock up boy and watch suffer in name of justice, no?"

Sarah had the old Beretta, but it was too hard a shot in the dark. Too much risk of hitting Ollie. "I couldn't give two shits about you, Maxim, but Oliver Simpson can still face up to what he did. He can help people heal and ensure nothing like it ever happens again. Repentance can make a difference, something you would know nothing about."

"You want boy to apologise for killing hundreds of people? Ha! Such a thing is worthless, but okay. You leave now, or I kill boy and you never get your worthless apology."

The two men standing with Maxim tossed their guns on the ground and put up their hands. Their nerves had abandoned them as it became clear there was no possible escape.

Sarah grinned. "And I thought you only hired idiots, Maxim. Looks like at least two of your men have common sense. There's no way out of this for you. It's over. You're just a footnote. Time to leave things to the real criminals."

Maxim glared at his surrendering men. "I will bury the both of you alive." He turned back to Sarah. "And you, I will make my whore until mind breaks."

"Sorry, Maxim, it takes someone a little taller to blow my mind."

"I... I will kill you."

"Yeah, yeah. Look around you, Maxim. Your tiny empire is in flames. Even if, through some miracle, you get away, we have so much evidence against you that you won't be able to take a shit without an armed response turning up at your door."

"Then I shall die here, right after I kill boy."

Ollie sobbed. "Just let him kill me. I don't care. Sarah, please, just let it be over."

Sarah considered her options. Ollie Simpson was either getting out of this alive – or not. Both options sucked. Whatever happened, he would forever be known as a mass murderer beyond forgiveness. His life had ended this morning, sitting in front of a monitor.

Maxim has no chance of getting out of here, even with a hostage. He must know that.

He's too calm.

Sarah glanced at Howard. He had his sidearm raised but didn't seem worried – why would he be? – yet something felt wrong here. She studied Maxim for a moment, increasingly bothered by his tranquillity. Then it made sense. "You have more men coming, don't you?"

Maxim readjusted his grip on Ollie, making sure the boy's body prevented him from being shot. Then he grinned, a gold tooth flashing in the gloom. "A simple phone call, my sweetheart. All we need to do is wait. I will enjoy cutting off your tits."

Sarah shook her head and sighed. Maxim must have made a phone call once he had realised the fight was going badly. How many men were now on their way? How heavily armed?

He's going to keep this standoff going until his thugs arrive and slaughter us. He's safe, because we are the good guys and we won't take a shot while he has a hostage.

She turned to Howard. "Call in backup of our own."

He nodded. "I'm on it, but I don't know how long it will take."

"Don't worry, it's only a precaution. Once Maxim is dead, we'll get these two prisoners to call off his reinforcements." She nodded at the two men who had put their hands up. Both appeared confused.

Maxim scoffed. "You cannot kill me. You are weak woman serving weak country."

Sarah raised the old Beretta and pulled the trigger.

The woods lit up.

The bullet struck Oliver Simpson right through the eyeball, killing him instantly and passing right through into Maxim's chest. Ollie's lifeless body slid out of Maxim's grasp and crumpled against the floor, while Maxim wiped at his face frantically, blinded by blood and brain matter. He held onto the Colt Python, but he was too stunned to use it.

Sarah took aim and fired again, shooting Maxim in the middle of the throat.

Maxim fell back against the incline, still practically standing because it was almost perpendicular. He grabbed at his throat, gargling and fighting for breath, his wickedness replaced by terror. Sarah moved in front of him and looked into his eyes while he died. It took less than a minute. She didn't miss a second, even to blink.

One more evil son-of-a-bitch dealt with. One more piece of my soul gone.

Out of interest, Sarah ejected the Beretta's clip and checked it. It was empty. Her last bullet had been meant for Maxim.

I won't ever fire another one.

Howard moved up beside Sarah, his breathing shallow. "What the hell did you do? You shot the kid. He was a hostage."

"I gave him mercy, trust me."

"Sarah..."

A dozen rifles pointed her way, so she dropped the empty Beretta on the ground and put her hands above her head. She knelt down in the moss and tried not to pass out.

It was time to see just how much her reputation would protect her.

But whatever happened, she was finished at the MCU.

She looked over at Oliver Simpson, the youngest person she had ever killed. A boy she had saved from a life of being a mass murderer in prison with a conscience. It had been a mercy. The last mercy she had left to give.

I'm done with death.
I'm done with this life.

ONE MONTH LATER...

Sarah was surprised to find Howard waiting outside the Home Office headquarters in Marsham Street, but it was a *pleasant* surprise. The chilly weather of February had given way to a March more hopeful of warmth, yet he wore his long grey woollen coat and a pair of leather gloves. His face and hair were once again neat and trimmed. "Did they set a date for your execution?" he said.

She shrugged. "The committee concluded negligence exacerbated by extreme fatigue. I said I was aiming for Maxim and took a bad shot. They couldn't prove anything intentional. Six months suspension and thirty hours of mandatory counselling. Not bad, really."

Howard turned to face the other way, and they started walking side by side down the street. "Could have been worse," he said. "Did you accept the punishment?"

"I accepted the counselling, but not the suspension. I told them I quit instead."

He stopped walking. "You quit? Are you sure that was the right call? What would the MCU be without you?"

She stopped walking, too, and she grabbed his hand. "There

probably won't be an MCU left after what Thomas did. Part of the reason they just went so easy on me in there is because they're terrified of me making a fuss. The evidence you and I gave them sent a shockwave through the entire government. Once it gets out to the public there'll be a mass culling – a herd of scapegoats. The Home Secretary has already been charged with corruption offences, and it's going to be a long while before Maxim's entire operation is exposed. I just... I just don't have the strength left in me to weather that storm. I'm done. And that's okay."

"It's not okay with me. I brought you into the MCU. I feel responsible for all you've been through."

"Hey, listen to me. You saved my life by bringing me into the MCU. That day, when you found me losing my shit in a bank, was one of the best days of my life. It gave me a chance to rewrite all the wrongs of my past – Hesbani, Al-Sharir, my dad – but it also gave me back my future. I'm tired and troubled, but I'm strong and proud. And loved."

Howard nodded. "You are. The whole of law enforcement worships you."

"I don't care about that. I'm talking about you and Jessica, Mandy and Mattock. You all mean the world to me, and if I didn't have you all in my life I would have become something dark and twisted. Your positivity... Jessica's no-nonsense way of dealing with my bullshit... You've each helped me get to where I needed to be."

"And where's that?"

"Home – but not a physical place. I'm finally at home being myself, and that's why it's time for me to leave. The MCU is a great place for penance, but I'm done trying to atone. No more chasing down evil and risking my life. I'm going to spend my future doing what *I* want to do, and maybe actually being kind to myself. I want to smile without a smirk, to sleep without keeping one eye open."

"I understand, and whatever you need, I'm here for you, but people are going to miss you."

She shrugged. "For a while, but life will go on. The MCU was a big part of my life, but I don't want it to be the *only* part." She looked at her watch, almost 5PM. "Anyway, I want to get a drink. You in?"

"Actually, I was here to ask you the same. We all wanted to be here for the results of your hearing, and we decided to have a few drinks to celebrate."

"How did you know I would get off lightly?"

He frowned but smiled at the same time. "Because there wasn't a single person who gave evidence against you – and the new director of the MCU made a case personally on your behalf."

"Jessica went to bat for me?"

"Of course she did. She gave the committee a right dressing down. Told them the Home Office would have remained a cesspool of corruption if not for you, and that Thomas Gellar and Maxim Ivanov would have brought the country to its knees eventually without your intervention.

"Wow. Then I definitely owe her a drink."

"But that's not what the whole celebration is for. It's also for—"

"Hey!"

Sarah and Howard turned around, looking back towards the Home Office. Rebecca Simpson marched towards them down the pavement, face red with fury. She was glaring right at Sarah. "You killed him," she shouted. "You shot my boy. My only child."

Howard went to step in front of Sarah, but she held him back. Instead, she stepped forward to face the woman down. "Rebecca?"

"Don't you call me that. Don't you dare say my name. You killed my boy... my buttercup." The woman was sobbing almost hysterically. She reached into her coat.

Sarah leapt forward and grabbed her forearm. "Rebecca? I

don't know what you have buried in there – a knife, a gun, or whatever – but you need to throw it away. I know what I took from you, but this won't give it back. Ollie told me about his sister. I know how much you've lost already."

The woman fought to reach into her coat, glaring at Sarah the whole time. "He wouldn't have told you that."

Sarah breathed in the woman's sadness. It came off her like perfume. "He did tell me. He tried to explain why he did it. He was a mixed-up, troubled kid that made a mistake. If he hadn't been so intelligent, his mistake would have been smaller and he would still be with us."

"They're calling him a monster. They're calling you a hero for shooting him."

Sarah shrugged. "Fuck 'em. The newspapers don't know shit. I met Ollie; I know he never meant to hurt anyone. He was angry and depressed, but he was just trying to find some meaning in his life. What happened was a tragic accident, but it was a mistake he would never have been free of. I shot your son because I wanted to save him from spending sixty years rotting in prison. Sixty years that would have twisted him into something miserable and unrecognisable. He wanted to die, Rebecca. He understood the alternative and wanted no part of it. I just wish..." She shook her head. "I just wish there had been any other way to save him, but there wasn't. Ollie was a good kid."

Mrs Simpson nodded, but her sobbing increased. Finally, she stopped trying to reach into her coat. "He was!" she blubbered. "He was a *good* boy, and I... I let him down. After his sister died... I should have been there for him more."

"You did your best, I'm sure, but sometimes it just isn't enough. The world has a way of biting the innocent. You think the people of flight CAS8-96 deserved what happened to them?"

"I keep seeing their faces," Rebecca said, her voice wispy and hollow. "Their photographs have been all over the news. Children. Even a baby. People throw eggs at my house. They post *things* through my letterbox."

Sarah nodded. "Eventually the jackals will move onto fresher meat, and your life will... stop hurting so much. The only thing I can tell you is that taking your pain out on me won't help. You might think you'll feel better killing me, but I promise you that I showed kindness to your son. I never gave up on him, and when I pulled the trigger, it was because it was what he wanted."

Rebecca bared her teeth. "Are you telling me he *wanted* to die?"

"Yes. I'm telling you he asked me to end his life, and when I decided to do so, it was because I knew it was the kindest thing to do. You might disagree, and as his mother, you have a right to retribution, but I hope you can find it in your heart to forgive me. Rebecca, I'm going to let go of your arm now, okay? If you want to hurt me, I won't stop you. My advice, though, is to go home to your husband and try to deal with your pain another way."

Sarah let go of the woman's arm. She sensed Howard behind her and knew he would probably leap into action if something happened, but she held true to her word and stood still, waiting for Rebecca's decision.

Please don't shoot me.

Rebecca's arm lingered inside her coat. Her expression went back and forth between anger and sadness and rage. There were several moments when Sarah saw the woman make up her mind and choose vengeance, but eventually something else won out. She withdrew her arm and wailed in pain. Sarah stepped forward and grabbed her, pulling her into a hug and telling her, "You didn't fail him, Rebecca. He had a conscience. He was decent. The world may think of him as a monster, but they don't get to tell you how to feel. It's okay to keep on loving him. It's okay to keep on living."

Rebecca shoved Sarah away, then turned and marched back down the street.

Sarah stood for a moment, until Howard let out a gasp. "Jesus. Do you think we should call someone? What if she goes off on someone else?"

"She won't. That was the top of the mountain for her. Now she has to start the slow, painful descent towards something resembling an ordinary life. I just hope she makes it to the bottom in one piece."

"I can't even imagine what's she going through. Her son is the most hated person in Britain."

"That's why it's better Oliver Simpson is dead." She shook herself, wondering if that was her last life used up. "I could *really* use that drink now."

Howard nodded. "Follow me."

It was one of the few London pubs not yet updated with a garish theme. Sarah enjoyed studying the horse brasses on the walls and the stains on the worn red carpet. Howard led her to a table near the back, where she found all of the people who mattered to her. They all stood and raised their glasses as she approached.

"To Sarah," said Jessica, out of her lab coat and in a shimmering blue blouse. "Bulletproof and Teflon-coated. I would sooner see the MCU burn than have you gone."

Sarah grimaced. "Well, I kinda quit my job. I'm done."

For a moment Jessica seemed mortified, but then she shrugged and raised another toast. "Well, here's to me coming up with a pay increase that you won't be able to refuse."

"Or a retirement party with all the honours," said Mattock.

Sarah smirked. "Congratulations on your new position, Director."

"Ah, don't it just feel good on the lips? Director Jessica Bennett, MD, Phd."

"It sounds perfect. Palu is probably toasting you from Heaven."

"He was Sikh," said Howard.

"Toasting you from nirvana, then." She narrowed her eyes at Howard. "Is that right?"

"Not even close. What are you having?"

"Lager. Pint."

"Coming right up."

Sarah sat down next to Mandy while Howard got her beer. Around the table were Mandy, Mattock, Jessica, and Matt. Matt's presence was a surprise, so Sarah quizzed him. "How come you're here?"

"Several reasons," he said with a smile. "Firstly, Howard contacted me and told me you were having a small remembrance for Thomas Gellar."

"He wasn't all bad," Jessica added.

Sarah nodded. "He wasn't. He just lost his way, made too many mistakes, and mistakes have a way of ruling the plans we have for ourselves. Just look at Oliver Simpson."

Matt nodded. "I saw Thomas sacrifice himself to try to help you. I never knew the man myself, but it felt right to raise a glass to him. The other reason I'm here, though, is because I applied to join the MCU."

"And I accepted," said Jessica. "While I do love my young analysts, it's nice to hire someone with a little bit of the old school about them."

"I have to admit," said Matt, "part of the reason I applied was because of the chance of working with you, Sarah. Are you sure you won't consider staying?"

"My mind's made up" – she looked at Jessica – "and no amount of money will change it. You should definitely work for the MCU, though. It needs honest men."

Matt blushed. "Okay, then I guess I'll try to live up to the high bar you've set."

Mattock placed his pint glass down on the table. It looked like he had lost a lot of weight, and he moved stiffly, but the smile on his face suggested he was in high spirits. "Looks like this is our joint retirement party then, lass. Maybe we can start a canasta team."

Sarah wrinkled her nose. "No thanks, I don't like dancing."

"No, it's... never mind. I'm just glad to see you quitting while there's still some life in you. You don't want to wait until you're all battered and old like I bloody well am. The soddin' bastards almost fitted me with a colostomy bag. Thank the heavens it never came to that."

Everyone laughed.

"I'll be around," said Sarah. "I may be leaving, but everyone at this table is my family. And I still need my family."

"You'll never be shot of us, lass."

"No way," said Mandy. "I'll happily be your honorary driver from time to time. Although I'm hanging up my keys. Jessica made me deputy director."

Sarah spluttered. "You're kidding me!"

Mandy's face fell. "You don't think I'm up to it?"

"I think the role requires someone loyal, hardworking, and willing to do whatever it takes to keep agents alive in the field. Mandy, you're perfect for the job."

"I thought so too," said Jessica, sipping from her red wine.

Mandy blushed, his face like that of a giant teddy bear.

Howard returned with Sarah's drink. She downed half the pint in one go. It felt great to get tipsy without the fear of suddenly being called in to deal with a crisis. She would miss the job, but she was eager to find a new purpose in life.

One that lets me sleep whenever I want.

Christ, I still haven't caught up yet.

The fallout after Maxim Ivanov's death had been rapid, and Sarah had gone another eight hours without sleep before finally crashing at her flat in London. Then, fourteen hours later, she had awoken to a shite storm. The MCU had been suspended, pending a full investigation, and Thomas's entire life was in the process of being ripped wide open. The files he had told Sarah about in the high street bank security locker were recovered and analysed. They gave evidence about every facet of Maxim Ivanov's operations at home and abroad, and also exposed dozens of corrupt officials within UK government. While Thomas had been a bad guy, he had done everything in his power to one day redeem himself. The utter transparency of his files was the main reason the MCU had eventually reopened with Jessica as the new director. It was clear that no one had aided or abetted Thomas within the earthworm, and Sarah was grateful for that. It finally allowed her to forgive Thomas and move on.

The investigations went on and on, however, like the one into Sarah's unlawful shooting of Oliver Simpson. Luckily, as she had hoped, the MCU agents who witnessed the execution had spoken only in her defence. Not a single one had condemned her actions. That was why she knew she had to leave. If she continued as a senior officer in the earthworm after having illegally executed a hostage, then she would undermine everything the MCU stood for. She couldn't allow her agents to take orders from someone who had taken the law into their own hands. They needed to see that there were consequences for what she had done.

That was all in the past now, though. Tonight, she was unemployed and with a bunch of friends who were getting the drinks in. She needed this. Her life was just about to begin.

But it can begin tomorrow.

It was a little after eleven when Sarah stumbled out of the pub into the crisp night air. She needed a taxi before she fell asleep where she was standing. While she was moderately drunk, it was fatigue more than anything else calling her to her bed. The others were still inside, making merry, but she didn't want the night to drag on. She didn't want to risk booze-fuelled outpourings of the heart. She loved them all dearly and hoped they would remain a part of her life. If not, then she would at least always carry them in her memories.

What a ride.

Matt appeared on the pavement beside her. "Think I might call it a night too," he said, "unless you fancy a nightcap?"

She smiled at him cheekily. "Are you asking me what I think you're asking me?"

"I don't know what you're thinking, but I was just thinking, now that we're not going to be colleagues, we could be something else."

She leant into him, chuckling. "Something else. Hmmm. Have you seen this face?"

"The scars just make you interesting. It's funny, but they kind of disappear after a while. They're just a part of you."

"Yeah, they are indeed. So, are you wanting to see if I have any more scars beneath my clothes, because I can tell you right now that I do. In fact, you shot me in the groin, so one of them is thanks to you."

He winked. "Let me make it up to you."

Matt was as handsome as they came. His short dark hair was greying at the temples, giving him a mature distinction, but his eyes were young and alive. His body looked rock hard beneath his T-shirt, and she longed to touch his chest. "You're pretty much the definition of a man, you know?"

He chuckled. "Thanks."

"I can imagine you and me together. We would really do some damage."

"I agree."

"But..."

"Oh dear." His lips fell at the corners and he shook his head. "I don't like that word."

"But..." She patted him on the arm. "You're not what I'm looking for. The darkness inside me would swallow you whole. I've been through way too much to make a guy like you happy."

"I've seen things too."

"Not like I have. I'm damaged."

"I'm willing to take you on."

She smirked and considered changing her mind. "I bet you are, but I've got about ten years of PTSD in my future and a whole lot of bottled-up trauma that I might never be able to talk about. I don't need the challenge of a new relationship on top of that."

He was silent for a moment, his brown eyes seeming to smoulder in the glare of the lights coming from the pub. Eventually, he nodded. "I suppose I get it. Just hearing about your exploits is traumatic enough, let alone living through them. I can't say I'm not disappointed, but I respect you too much to sulk. But if you ever change your mind, you know where to find me."

She nodded. "Yeah, doing my old job. You're welcome to it."

"Thanks."

"I'm just kidding. I wish you luck. You're quite a man, Matt. Jessica will be lucky to have you. Hey, she's single, you know – so long as you don't count cats."

"I'll bear that in mind." He let out a sigh and looked up at the night sky. "Okay then. I'm going to take my battered pride and take a walk home."

"We can share a taxi. There's no reason to—"

"No, please. That would be torture. Besides, I only live a few streets away. I'll see you around, Sarah. Take care of yourself."

"You too."

And that is why I was right to leave when I did. Yikes, did that just happen?

And did I just turn down the first sex I might have had in a very, very long time?

Oh well.

She was having no luck flagging down a taxi, so she decided to just head for the nearest rank and catch one there. When she turned, though, she noticed Howard standing in the doorway of the pub. "Hey," she said, pointing a finger gun at him. "What you doing out here? Spying on me? Because I'm out of the spy business."

"I came out to make sure you got a taxi, but instead I had to endure Matt crashing and burning. That was painful. Do you not think you should have given the guy a chance though? You deserve to be happy, Sarah."

"You're right, I do. Come stand with me."

He came over. "I'm going to miss you."

"Hey, I'm not going anywhere, so don't worry. You'll be too busy to miss me. Anyway, what with your sudden return from the dead, everyone at the MCU is going to kick your butt. We had a wake and everything. I think Cecily in IT named her kid after you."

"Probably best I won't be going back then."

"Huh? What are you talking about?"

"I just gave Jessica my resignation. Looks like she's had a lot of staff turnover this month. I feel a little bad for—"

"Wait? You quit? Why?"

"Same reason as you. The MCU is a place for penance, but I feel like I've given enough of myself to maybe do something else. I think I might go into teaching."

She smiled. "I think you would be really good at that. You're patient, kind. Maybe if I'd had teachers like you I wouldn't have felt like I needed to follow in my father's footsteps. Well, I won't try to talk you out of it, because, well, I'm in no position to. I just want you to be happy."

"I am happy," he said, nodding merrily. His eyes were a little bleary, but he was still himself. "It's a relief, you know. Like getting out of a war you were sure was going to kill you."

"A second chance?"

He nodded. "Maybe. More that I gave the parts of me I wanted to, but now I need to heal and see what's next. I'll always treasure my time at the MCU." He looked down at the ground, then glanced awkwardly at her. "I'll always treasure my time with you. You know, at first, I thought bringing you in was a mistake – you were so closed off and angry – but I was wrong. The only reason you were angry is because you care so much, and it turns out that bringing you in was the best thing I could have done. So many people are still alive today because of—"

She leant forward and kissed him. While it was clearly a shock for him, he quickly grabbed her and kissed her back. They squeezed their bodies together for two whole minutes before they broke apart.

"What was that?" Howard was blinking like he was trying to wake himself up.

"That was me looking after myself. You came out here to make sure I got a taxi, right?"

He blushed. "Well, yeah, I did."

"Want to make sure I get to my bed okay?"

Howard blushed, so much that he almost glowed. "Y-Yes, I do, but what about what you said to Matt? You don't have time for a new relationship."

She reached out and took both of his hands, rubbing her fingers over his scars on his damaged hand and raising it so that it rested on the scarred side of her face. She looked into his eyes, not at all self-conscious about her old wounds. "This isn't a new relationship, Howard. We've been together for seven years. We're a pair of wounded soldiers that have been through hell together. All of the darkness inside me, you have it too. I can be with you without having to explain my wounds because you were there for each one." She lowered his damaged hand and kissed it. "And I've been there for all of yours. We both need time to heal, but how about we do it together?"

He reached in and kissed her. "You never stop surprising me, you crazy death-seeking psycho."

"And you never stop making me feel safe, my heroic-jawed do-gooder." She took a breath, looking up at him. "I'm in love with you. Have been for a while. Your dying really brought it home to me. You could have been dead for real, and it would have been a waste. You would have been gone without me ever having the guts to open up and let you in."

"I love you too, Sarah. Let's put all the death behind us, yeah? Maybe it's time to start living."

She raised an eyebrow at him and squeezed his bum. "Oh, you have no idea, mister. Let's go find that taxi."

Sarah and Howard hurried down the path towards the taxi rank, laughing and joking the whole way. Ex-colleagues. Old friends. New lovers.

It was going to be a long, sweaty night.

I can sleep tomorrow, Sarah decided. *Or maybe the day after that. It's not like I have a job to get to.*

Don't miss out on your FREE Iain Rob Wright horror pack. Five terrifying books sent straight to your inbox.

No strings attached & signing up is a doddle.

Just visit iainrobwright.com

ALSO BY IAIN ROB WRIGHT

Animal Kingdom
AZ of Horror
2389
Holes in the Ground (with J.A.Konrath)
Sam
ASBO
The Final Winter
The Housemates
Sea Sick, Ravage, Savage
The Picture Frame
Wings of Sorrow
The Gates, Legion, Extinction, Defiance, Resurgence, Rebirth
TAR
House Beneath the Bridge
The Peeling
Blood on the bar
Escape!
Dark Ride
12 Steps
The Room Upstairs
Soft Target, Hot Zone, End Play, Terminal
The Spread: Book 1
The Spread: Book 2

Iain Rob Wright is one of the UK's most successful horror and suspense writers, with novels including the critically acclaimed, THE FINAL WINTER; the disturbing bestseller, ASBO; and the wicked screamfest, THE HOUSEMATES.

His work is currently being adapted for graphic novels, audio books, and foreign audiences. He is an active member of the Horror Writer Association and a massive animal lover.

www.iainrobwright.com
FEAR ON EVERY PAGE

For more information
www.iainrobwright.com
author@iainrobwright.com

Copyright © 2021 by Iain Rob Wright

Cover Artwork by Carl Graves at Extended Imagery

Editing by Richard Sheehan

All rights reserved.

No part of this book may be reproduced in any form or by any electronic or mechanical means, including information storage and retrieval systems, without written permission from the author, except for the use of brief quotations in a book review.

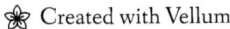 Created with Vellum

Printed in Great Britain
by Amazon